GAY IN MOSCOW

ADAM WYE

Anchor Mill Publishing

Anchor Mill Publishing

4/04 Anchor Mill

Paisley PA1 1JR

SCOTLAND

anchormillpublishing@gmail.com

Remembering a life-changing journey long ago, in the company of Rich Sybert, Jenny Hugget, Donald Matthew and more – including Peter Rowe, who later gave his life for others in a hostage-taking event in the Yemen in 1998

A Brother's Note

My brother Oliver died last year. His partner and he were killed in a road traffic accident. His partner was a man of his own age called Dickon. Yes, my brother was gay, which I am not – though I had no problem with his sexuality: it was just one of those things.

I had the task of sorting through Oliver's papers after his death. Among them I found an account of his meeting with Dickon nearly thirty years ago, which he had written within a few years of the events that he described.

The events that he described! Some were historically momentous, others deeply personal. He didn't shy away from frank details of his sex life ... which, naturally, I knew nothing about. I knew the outer shell, the carapace, of his story only. I didn't know the heart of it. But Oliver wrote about that heart. And about his own heart. He wore that heart of his on his sleeve in the story he wrote.

I thought the story wonderfully worth the reading. I thought it worth sharing with a wider audience. So here it is. I shall bow out now and let Oliver's story speak for itself. (Unedited. I've left everything, including the sex, as he wrote it. Readers who don't want to read certain things can simply skip.) And I won't be adding any comments of my own, or offering a tying-up chapter at the end. From now on all the words you read will be Oliver's own. You don't even need to know my name. Oliver doesn't mention it, and by the time you've arrived at the end of his story you won't even remember this introduction to it...

ONE

We first set eyes on each other at the check-in desk. I had arrived at Heathrow stupidly early: two hours before the flight. But it was going to be my first time aboard an aeroplane. I'd arrived on my own and I was very nervous. I'd be fine once I met up with the others, I told myself.

I mooched around the departures hall, looking at the rows of check-ins, the airline offices, the cafés and the banks. I'd never been in such a place. I was awed by it but fascinated by everything. I wanted to remember every last detail of this new experience. From time to time I wandered past the check-ins. The Aeroflot Moscow flight wasn't written up yet. I couldn't help noticing as I passed and re-passed those desks that someone else seemed to be doing the same thing as I was. I noticed him because … I'm going to try to be totally honest in this account of things and I'll start being honest at once … because I found him hugely attractive.

He was a few inches taller than I was, and very slim and lean. Not scrawny though (I was the scrawny, bony one) but elegantly slender like a greyhound or a racehorse. His hair was shiny black and his complexion tending towards olive. His eyes were big and brown and lustrous. He had full lips and a nose that was almost retroussé, and his cheekbones were high and finely sculpted. He was wearing blue jeans like I was, though he had moccasins on his feet – which I thought more dashing than my cheap trainers. Like me he was carrying a biggish hold-all and wore a backpack on his leather-jacketed shoulders.

I noticed all this because I couldn't not do. Not only did I find his looks very appealing; our paths crossed again and again as I waited for the Moscow check-in desk to declare itself. And for that reason he noticed me too. After a while we gave each other little complicit smiles as we silently walked past each other. I had no idea whether he was also waiting for the Moscow check-in to open but I rather wished he could be.

Then two things happened at once. Three of my university friends hove into sight, waving to me and laughing their greetings, and the sign went up at two of the check-in desks: *Moscow,* and the number and departure time of the Aeroflot flight. My arriving friends and I converged on the desk – and so did the guy I'd been admiring on and off for the past thirty minutes.

He spoke to us, addressing us as a group. 'Are you part of the Durham lot?' he asked, a little shyly. We said we were and introduced ourselves. 'I'm Dickon – from Edinburgh,' the new guy said.

'I'm Oliver,' I said, and we shook hands. Presumably Dickon also shook hands with the three others but I have no memory of that.

Dickon didn't speak with a Scottish accent. His speech was southern English like my own. When he'd said he was from Edinburgh he'd meant that he was at university there, not that it was his home town. This planned visit to Russia was, after all, a university student trip.

'Perhaps we'd better stay here and wait for the others,' I said. 'That's what the letter said.'

The others nodded but Dickon said, 'We can at least check ourselves in first. Get rid of our suitcases. Then wait for the others without our arms dropping off.' His was an improvement on my original idea, I had to admit. 'That makes sense,' I said, and beamed a smile at Dickon. I had no way of measuring my own smiles: I rarely saw them. Though I'd been told they were pretty good. I tried never to think about that; I didn't want them to become too calculated. But the one I gave Dickon just then must have been a good one, because he beamed a beautiful one back.

We ended up scattered around the aeroplane. It was an Ilyushin Il-62, the card in the pocket informed me: a jet with four tail-mounted engines. Its name was disconcerting. Too close to *illusion*. Now you see it, now you don't. It had a famously bad accident record. At least I had a window seat. I would see something of the countryside before we went down.

We didn't get far at our first attempt. We taxied a little way, then parked up near a hangar. We would be delayed for an hour, the stewardess informed us with a stern face. A little later she brought glasses of water on trays for all of us. 'Glass of water,' she announced in English. I found the glass interesting; it had an attractive, bulbous shape.

I didn't speak to the couple next to me. They spoke Russian to each other on the rare occasions they did speak and I assumed they spoke no English. Lunch was served while we waited on the tarmac. Happily a glass of white wine came with it. Then at last we were off. We lifted off smoothly and a moment later the grey skies of London swallowed us.

And followed us. For two hours there was nothing to see except the tops of clouds. I tried to turn them into landscapes of shifting mountains and warring armies, or wrestling dragons with steaming breath. Then suddenly the sky parted and showed us a sea and a coast. The sea was grey. Slow-moving lines of greyish white rolled shoreward, far apart viewed from above, to vanish mournfully on a beach of grey sand. A grey city stood beside the sand, with a harbour and, a little way inland, an airport – a pattern of grey runways on grey grass. It all looked depressed and cold.

'We are crossing the coast of Russia over the city of Riga,' the stewardess announced severely. I just about remembered that Riga was the capital of Latvia, so the sea we were looking at was the icy Baltic. Not everybody believed that Latvia was part of Russia at all. Never mind; from now on I had a view to look out at. For nearly two hours I looked down on snow-covered pine forests and vast lakes among them. My parents had a recording of a Sibelius symphony whose cover depicted just such a scene. But that didn't go on for two hours.

I learned later that passenger planes usually descend gradually from cruising height over a period of twenty-five minutes. This was not the way with Aeroflot, apparently. We did it in ten. 'We are landing at Moscow,' the stewardess announced, bracing her feet against the floor as the plane tipped stomach-knottingly down. There was no sign of Moscow outside the window. Not a house, not a road. Just continuing pine trees. Perhaps the city was on the other side.

Then the airport appeared, a sudden big clearing among the trees. The grass beside the runway had died down beneath the winter snow. There was nothing green to be seen except the dark pine trees beyond the perimeter. Where there had been grass at Heathrow, here there was a patchwork of slush, melt-water and black mud, among which waddled – and sometimes flapped away – a population of grey-hooded crows. Welcome to Moscow, I told myself as we landed. There was no-one else to say it to me.

They searched our suitcases thoroughly at Customs, taking everything out and putting it back. I'd brought The Political Writings of Saint Augustine. They took a good long look at that before re-packing it. The unusual-looking lady at the next table had a case containing reams of silk. As the bright-coloured fabrics were unravelled, gold watches tumbled out. One of our party counted them, he told me later. They numbered a hundred and twelve.

Once we were released our guide appeared: a bright young blonde girl, only a few years older than most of us. She introduced herself as Natasha and led us towards an unheated bus. At last we left the pine forests behind us and travelled along a pot-holed road. The suburbs were built of wood: the houses poor and, though they were well-endowed with windows the windows had no curtains at them.

Our hotel was on the northern side of the city – that was the same side as the airport – and was not difficult to get to: there was very little traffic in the streets. The first thing we noticed about the hotel was its glass porch: a sort of decompression chamber between the outside cold and the heated interior. It was early April but the outdoor cold was very much in evidence. The second thing was the discovery that we would be four to a room. There were eighteen of us, half boys, half girls, and it took a few minutes to work out the details of who would share with whom.

Saying that half of us were boys was perhaps flattering to the four academics who were part of the party: two from my university, Durham, and two from York. I ended up sharing a room with the two Durham dons – one I didn't know, but he was young and looked like being fun – the other was my slightly older history tutor, a rather aloof and formal person: he wasn't someone I'd ever imagined myself sharing a bedroom with. But none of that mattered in the slightest. The fourth member of our room group was Dickon. We hadn't spoken to each other since our first encounter at the Heathrow check-in. Now, quite by chance, we were going to be roommates. I was over the moon about that.

I hadn't yet admitted to myself that I was gay. Admittedly all the evidence to date pointed to the probability that I was. I'd had occasional fumblings with other boys and loved it. I'd had no sexual contact with females, not even experimental kisses, and I didn't regret that a bit. If I fancied someone that someone was always of the male sex, and when I masturbated myself to sleep at night the sexy images that came into my mind – all right, I sometimes hauled them there deliberately – were always of blokes.

I foresaw a problem here. I wasn't sure how I would be able to manage this – I mean the wanking thing – when sharing a room with three other guys. That one of them was the beautiful Dickon was no less of a problem than that one of the others was Doctor Cotton, my tutor in medieval history. I tried to console myself with the thought that Dickon, who looked about the same age as I was, might be having similar thoughts as he unpacked his bags across the small room from me (our bottoms were about a foot apart) and having the same problem to surmount. But we'd only exchanged a few sentences to date and had only just met this morning; the logistical problems surrounding wanking in shared accommodation wasn't a subject I was going to raise with him. Certainly not yet.

We went downstairs for dinner. The restaurant was

self service. There were three courses but no choice. We began with a salad that was really quite good: heavy on gherkins and beetroot, with dill and tomato among the chopped lettuce. The pinkish stew that followed it... I had read Nineteen-Eighty-Four. I knew all about pinkish stew. Now I knew why George Orwell had included his evidently unforgettable experience of it in his account of totalitarian squalor. I wished now that I'd had a double portion of salad instead.

After we'd eaten there was a group meeting, at which Natasha set out the plans for the next few days. Our time in Russia looked like being very organised. We would be shepherded from place to place under Natasha's benevolent but watchful eye; there would not be too many opportunities for us to strike out on our own. Natasha answered our many questions then bade us all a friendly goodnight. We would be setting off early the next day.

The room in which the meeting was held contained a bar, I couldn't help noticing. Two women stood behind it like sentries. They were not doing anything, not even talking to each other. It seemed to me that their function was to guard the bottles of liquor on the shelves behind them rather than to serve customers with it. My theory appeared to be confirmed when, as soon as Natasha had left us, a number of us headed over to them.

None of us young people spoke Russian. But we knew how to point. And smile. And two of the others knew the word for please, which is *pazhalusta*. It did us no good. No drinks were forthcoming. The staff responded to our gestures with one of their own. They smacked their hands, palm down, on the counter in front of them. Quite loudly. And they didn't smile while they were doing it.

We were rescued by one of the dons from York, who came over to us. He did speak a certain amount of Russian, he had already let us know, and had been to Russia several times before. 'In Russia,' he told us, 'you put your money on the counter first. Then you name your drink. Then you get it.' He addressed a few incomprehensible words to the women behind the bar and withdrew. Gratefully we followed his instructions and a minute later had all been served with the drink of our choice. I opted for red wine. Russian wine. I was curious to know what it would taste like. It tasted fine. But I had already found that all wine did.

'So, Oliver...' I nearly jumped. A pair of beautiful brown eyes were peering into mine from a height about three inches above the level of my own. 'What brings you to Russia?'

'I could ask you the same question, Dickon.'

'I got it in first.'

The others had taken their drinks back to their seats. Dickon and I were the last men standing at the bar counter. 'OK,' I said. 'I loved the strangeness of it. The awful tragedies of its history... Fascinated by books and pictures. I wanted to see it for myself. Then this chance came up...'

Dickon was nodding slowly. 'Exactly the same here,'

he said.

'You're the only one here from Edinburgh?' I checked.

'Right. And from Durham...?'

'Six of us,' I said. 'Six students. Then there's our two roommates, of course.'

'Do they both teach you?' Dickon asked.

'Doctor Cotton does,' I said. 'Doctor Peters is in the maths department. I met him for the first time today.'

'So you're reading history like me,' Dickon said.

'Like you,' I said. The two words tasted sweet.

'How well do you know Jenny?' Dickon asked. Jenny was one of the girls in the Durham party. I found her about as attractive as any girl I'd ever met.

'We're in the same tutorial group,' I said. 'I've known her a year and a half. She's great.' I saw Dickon's eyebrows rise. 'Nothing like that, though,' I said. 'We're not...'

'Does she have a boyfriend?'

'There's two or three guys keen on her at Durham. She keeps them at arm's length, I think. I think there's someone at home in the vacations...' I might have been making that up. Dickon's interest in Jenny was ever so slightly wounding. I didn't want to feel it that way, but I did. I wasn't happy to go on and on talking about her. I hoped one of us would change the subject.

'That was a hell of a landing today,' Dickon said, abruptly doing just that.

'Don't I know,' I said. 'Was it your first flight?'

'No,' said Dickon. 'I've flown to a few places.'

'It was my first flight,' I said. The words came out as though I was apologising for the fact.

TWO

Bedtime was an odd experience. An unexpected assortment of four males undressing together. We all turned our backs on one another as we stripped off and got into our pyjamas. Well, I presume we all turned our backs... I can only say for certain that I know I did. I had the bed opposite Dickon's. Doctor Cotton's bed was against the same wall as Dickon's was, foot to foot, while I shared a wall with the other, younger don, Doctor Peters. Doctor Peters, who was still in his twenties, was quite unfazed by the experience, and seemed rather amused by it. Doctor Cotton, though, seemed to find it a distressing one. I glanced quickly at him, transformed by a pair of green pyjamas – he who I was accustomed to see lecturing at the reading desk in formal jacket and bow tie, with a gold watch on a chain in his breast pocket – and said a friendly goodnight.

'Goodnight,' he replied, then bounced into his bed, said, 'Hell,' between clenched teeth and pulled the covers up over his head.

I exchanged a look with Dickon as we both climbed, pyjama-clad, into our own beds. 'Sleep well,' I said to him.

'Sleep well, Oliver,' he said from inside his own bed. It was the second time I'd heard my name on his lips. I seemed to taste it on my own at the same instant and the sensation was sweet.

We were all up and dressed, and downstairs, queuing for breakfast, by eight thirty the next morning. Breakfast was interesting. There was a big sticky bun to be eaten with a boiled egg, there was salami and bread, and there was yoghurt. There was tea in tall hot glasses. No milk was offered with it, and there was certainly no sign of any slices of lemon – something I'd always believed was the very thing that made Russian tea Russian. But the tea had an excellent flavour (it was *chai* in Russian, it rhymed with sky) and there were oblong slabs of sugar to put in it. These 'double-cubes' were almost impossible to dissolve, though. Nor could you break them with your fingers or a spoon. They seemed to have been formed under unimaginable compression, like diamonds in a coal mine, and lingered at the bottom of our tea-glasses, despite all our hopeful stirrings and proddings with spoons until the last mouthful of liquid was drunk.

Natasha arrived with a bus to take us into the city centre to have a look around. Our potholed road was the route the trolley-buses took between the Exhibition Park of National Achievements and Red Square. It was the trolley-bus we would need to take, Natasha said, if we were on our own in the city centre and wanted to get back to the hotel. The roads were pot-holed, certainly, but they were eerily traffic-free.

Once we'd arrived in central Moscow Natasha was eager to show us the newest architectural gems: huge blocks of flats of great ugliness, vast government buildings like giant but somehow squat, square-sided space rockets, with pointed tops and boosters at the four corners. We appealed to her to let us stop and look at the crumbling, beautiful old churches we passed, with their peeling onion domes. Natasha couldn't quite understand our interest in these relics of the old bad times, but in the end she gave in and let us look – and photograph – our fill.

We went back to our hotel for lunch. 'What do you think this is?' Dickon asked me, as he prodded at a lumpen slab of meat.

'It's cold, for one thing,' I said. 'And so are the chips. But I've never seen steak with such big grain as that. Almost sweet tasting...' And a bit gelatinous.

'Know what?' said Dickon. 'I reckon it's horse.'

We ate it, whatever it was. It didn't taste too bad, to be honest. We washed it down with glasses of what Natasha called gas-water. I couldn't help thinking that the English expression for it had more charm about it.

We were back on the bus before we knew it. Natasha took us to a gallery to look at some *art*. There were endless portraits from the eighteenth, nineteenth and twentieth centuries, of people whose names meant nothing to us. Only a few of them really stood out. And then suddenly we were in a different world. Rooms full of wonderful icons that dated back half a millennium. Just paint on flat surfaces. No hologram techniques had been available to their creators. And yet as you peered into them you saw perspectives that stretched back, seemingly to infinity, of space and time and human thought.

And then it was supper time, back at our hotel. Macaroni with some sort of meat fried in batter. Nobody dared to think what kind of meat it was. At the end of a cold dark day it tasted all right.

At the end of the meal one of the two dons from York – his name was Professor Sykes – announced that he was going into the city centre to have a look at Red Square by night. Anyone who wanted to go along was welcome to join him, though he wouldn't be giving a conducted tour or leading a party. I thought that was fair enough. I looked across the table at Dickon. 'Want to go for that?' I asked.

'Why not?' he said. A few minutes later some eight or ten of us had straggled along the dark street towards the main road and caught the trolley-bus.

There was no conductor. You put your coins – a ridiculously small number of kopeks – into a perspex-sided honesty box at the top of the bus's inside steps. These were the People's trolley-buses and the People's kopeks, and the People sat all around, glaring at you and glaring at the honesty box, making sure you actually put in the coins. How to describe the People? They wore a hard look each, as if they had eaten something indigestible but could now do nothing about it. And in a way that was the case. The Revolution of 1917 had improved the lot of the poorest classes enormously. But that had been a single step. No further improvements had taken place since. The Western world had grown exponentially richer in the sixty-nine years since, despite the calamities of two World Wars. In Russia that increase in prosperity hadn't come about. At least not yet. Though now a new man was in power in the Kremlin. Mikhail Gorbachev. A new broom, a reformer, a darling of the West. But he'd only been in place for a year so far. His sweeping changes had not yet impinged on the pockets or the outlook of the women on the Moscow trolley-bus.

We got off at the corner of Red Square and walked into the floodlit centre of it. It seemed the most natural as well as the most beautiful thing that Dickon and I were walking shoulder to shoulder. 'How old are you?' I suddenly asked.

'Nineteen,' Dickon said.

'Me too,' I told him. 'Have you ever seen anything like this in your life?'

'No,' Dickon said.

A single snowflake fell from nowhere. It pirouetted in the air in front of us then landed on the cobbled surface at our feet. It stayed there. It didn't melt. It was big: bigger than a Cornflake but whiter than white. A similar-sized friend then joined it. A moment later the floodlit square was a whirling mass of flakes. There were few people about, apart from our group. We stood transfixed, enchanted by the sights around us. Ahead of us rose the great cathedral of St Basil, its domes and spires like whorls of ice-cream in cones, many-coloured and sparkling with light. To the left stood the monumental department store called GUM, now closed for the night. And on our right ran the long red wall of the Kremlin with its picturesque battlements shaped like whittled wood clothes-pegs, split end uppermost. Armed guards stood at its entrance gates while churches and other buildings peered over the tops of the battlements at us, visions of medieval splendour, gold and white.

And white. The cobbles were covered within a minute, whited out, and our feet made only temporary tracks in the snowy carpet as we walked. We had seen grey Moscow in the daytime, had been infected by its drabness and felt downcast. Now we were seeing Moscow in the snow-time, seeing the awesome beauty of it floodlit at night. It was like being inside a poem or a painting; we were willing captives of the place. With the snow's magic brushstrokes Moscow had come to life for us. We were seeing it as it was meant to be seen, feeling it as it was meant to be felt.

'When's your birthday?' I asked Dickon.

'May the seventh,' he said.

'Mine's June the seventh,' I said. He was exactly a month older than me. *Within a month, a little month…*

'OK,' said Dickon. His voice sounded as though he was as struck by our closeness in age as I was. 'That's something we're not going to forget.'

I was in the most beautiful place I'd ever been, with the most beautiful person I'd ever met. I was aching with the wonder of the moment and almost unable to breathe, fearing that I might blow the fragile experience out of existence like a candle flame or like a snowflake. Dickon and I were both wearing gloves; mine were woollen, his were leather. I wanted at that moment to put my hand in his and clasp his fingers, but I dared not.

We drifted past the snow-swept, heavily guarded, entrance to Lenin's tomb. We circled St Basil's and its twisted ice-cream tops seemed to curl round to follow us, while the dancing snowflakes blew in their white billions around its cross-crowned peaks. We were all almost speechless with the wonder of it. But then Dickon spoke. To me. Just to me. 'This is what we came here for, isn't it?' He made it sound like a real question. As though he was diffidently unsure whether I would agree with him or not.

I did agree. It seemed terribly important that he knew I did. 'You're telling me,' I said. My answer clearly pleased him because he half turned and smiled his pleasure, almost his relief, into my face. I smiled back at him. 'You can call me Oli if you like,' I said.

'And you can call me Dick.' He sniggered after he'd said that, obviously thinking about another meaning of the word dick.

I sniggered too. 'I will,' I said.

By the time we left Red Square it had been snowing

for an hour and the soft white carpet was a foot deep. We went into the Metropol Hotel to have a coffee and to warm up. None of us students would have been brave enough, probably, to walk in there off the street. The Metropol was Moscow's oldest, grandest and most palatial hotel. We weren't sure of the rules yet, not sure what kinds of infringements would get us sent to Siberia without a trial first. But Professor Sykes and the other don from York were old hands in Moscow and had stayed at the Metropol in the past. They weren't intimidated, as the rest of us might have been, by the sentry-like flunkeys or the glittering chandeliers that lit the lounges and reception areas. I looked about me. This was very different from our own hotel that was actually more like a hostel. The Metropol was very splendid. I could get used to this, I thought.

There were more chandeliers for afterwards, because we took the metro back. It was almost a grander experience than the Metropol. Each long escalator dived down beneath chandeliers in serried ranks. Wizened old women in black sat on chairs at top and bottom. Their job was to push the stop button if anyone fell and injured themselves. We never saw this happen. The old women were paid for sitting there, like museum staff. Probably they weren't paid much. I began to understand how Russia managed to have full employment.

The escalators decanted us into a cathedral-like space, brightly painted and brightly lit. There were yet more chandeliers high above our heads. There were no platforms to be seen, but people were heading for the long side walls in which rows of sliding doors were set, like the entrances to lifts. When the doors slid open – hey presto – they were to reveal a train standing behind the wall, its doors open and ready to receive us just like a lift's inner portal. The journey back involved a change of lines. And that in itself involved more chandeliers...

We stamped the snow from our cold feet inside the decompression-chamber of the lobby of our hotel. There was a sense of anticlimax as we said goodnights to one another, but there was not much to be done except go to bed. It was eleven o'clock and the hotel bar was closed. Together Dickon and I climbed the stairs.

Doctor Cotton and Doctor Peters hadn't joined our group. They'd gone into town as a separate party with two of the older girls. The idea of Doctor Cotton going out on a date – even a double date – was a new thing for me to get my head round. I was still a prisoner of the schoolboy idea that people belonged in one context only. Parents were parents and nothing else, teachers were teachers only, and existed only to teach. That such people had feelings and might go out on the razz in a foreign city... I still had a lot to learn.

The two dons had not yet returned by the time Dickon and I got undressed for bed. Back to back again. Well, I know I had my back turned to Dickon. When I was securely fastened inside my pyjamas I turned to face him before climbing into my bed. The room wasn't big, the four beds almost filled it, so I found Dickon standing, tucked snugly into his own pyjamas within arms' reach of me.

24

I don't know how it happened. It didn't seem to be Dickon who initiated it; it didn't seem to be me. We were suddenly in each other's arms, exchanging a cosy goodnight hug. It lasted just a second or two. Neither of us made an attempt to kiss the other. But I felt Dickon's warm breath against my cheek, and smelt the toothpastey freshness of it in my nose. 'Goodnight Oli,' he said. He seemed almost to sing the words.

'Goodnight Dick,' I said to him and I felt my world turn upside down. We got into our separate beds and turned the lights off. Then we said goodnight again.

I lay in the darkness, feeling my heart thumping. My cock was hard and my mood was somewhere in the stratosphere. I wanted to wank. I wanted to do it with Dick, but obviously that was out of the question. Failing that I would have liked to do it all by myself under the sheet. I didn't dare, though. I lay awake for a bit, just feeling helplessly horny. I couldn't help wondering if Dickon was feeling the same. I didn't know how to find out; how I could ever find out. Dickon's feelings were a locked box to which I didn't have the key.

I fell asleep eventually. We nearly always do. I wasn't awoken by the return of Doctors Cotton and Peters. But they obviously did return, because in the morning there they were.

THREE

What's in a hug? A hug with any other guy would feel as sweet... And yet it would not. A hug isn't freighted with the intimacy of a kiss, but still it leaves an imprint. Conjure the memory of any particular hug in your experience and hey presto, the unique physicality of the person you shared it with will come to life in your arms as surely as Proust's memories flowed from the experience of dipping a Madeleine into his teacup.

Before that bedtime hug with Dickon my previous hug (not counting the farewell hug my mother had given me as I set out for the airport) had been with a guy named Mo.

Mo was short for Morgan, as I discovered soon after meeting him during Freshers' Week at the start of my first term at Durham. He was a handsome lad, I thought. He was the same modest height that I was, though he was sturdier and better developed muscularly. He had fine blond hair that was wavy, and piercing, though unthreatening, blue eyes. They were more than unthreatening: they were friendly and seemed to invite your trust and confidence. Mo and I were at the same college – which was known as Castle, because its main building was Durham Castle, high on its rock above the town. We had different sets of friends, studied different subjects and had different interests. Yet we were both interested in each other, and we found it easy to be on matey terms when we met by chance... Which because of the nature of college life happened some dozen times a day. If we passed in the street we nearly always stopped for a chat, however brief. What are you up to today? sort of thing. But in our second term something happened that rather shifted the tectonic plates.

It was the night of Castle Formal. That was the big social event of the college term. A dance, in formal attire, in the castle's Great Hall. A buffet supper laid out along the length of the Norman Gallery. Coffee and liqueurs, if you wanted, in the extravagantly Regency Senior Common Room. I had invited a girl from St Aidan's College. Her name was Adrienne.

I was fine with girls at dances. I was fine with girls in all social situations. I wasn't a bad kisser – and had been known to do this in depth from time to time. It was what might happen after those things that I couldn't bring myself to deal with. My dances and other social evenings ended, always, with me gallantly escorting the girl back to wherever she lived and a brief hug and kiss on the doorstep. This night was no exception.

I walked with Adrienne from the castle, across Palace Green, then down the lane beside the Music School that led to the riverside walk down to Prebends' Bridge. After that there was a short steep climb through woods, then by road, towards St Aidan's College, a rather splendid piece of modern architecture by Basil Spence, who had called it The Hand on the Hill.

I wasn't the only Castleman doing this walk that night. There were scores of us, walking our girlfriends, dance partners or whatever back to the women's colleges on the edge of town. In the middle of Prebends' Bridge I found I'd caught up with Mo. He was escorting a girl called Sadie back to her college, St Mary's. I'd already been introduced to Sadie. Our paths had already crossed that evening several times.

The four of us walked on together, companionably up the hill to where our ways divided. Mo and Sadie branched left to St Mary's; Adrienne and I climbed the shallow steps that led past a coppice to St Aidan's front door. As we climbed, the towers of Durham cathedral and its castle – the place where I slept – came into sight, floodlit, above the trees. It was a lovely thing and Adrienne and I stopped and looked at it for a minute before we said our goodnight and gave each other a chaste kiss before Adrienne disappeared indoors. Then I turned and went back down the steps, and the golden towers of cathedral and castle subsided slowly down behind the trees and disappeared, like jewels in a display case that was being closed.

When I came out into the road at the bottom of the steps there was Mo, by coincidence, passing that very spot on his return from St Mary's. It shouldn't have been surprising really: St Mary's and St Aidan's were the same distance from the place, and assuming you weren't going to go any farther with them, it took about the same amount of time to say goodnight to one girl as it did to say goodnight to another. But all the same... It was only much later that it crossed my mind that Mo might have timed his arrival at the bottom of Aidan's steps deliberately – hurrying a little, then slowing when the steps came into view, till he saw me appear.

'Hey there!' Mo greeted me.

'Well, well,' said I. Then we didn't say anything more but walked for a while in a silence that was not awkward but friendly and relaxed. We could have talked about the girls we'd just escorted back to college but we didn't. I didn't particularly want to. Neither, it appeared, did Mo. We left the road and walked down the broad track through the woods to the ancient Prebends' Bridge at the bottom. There were old-fashioned street-lamps among the trees. When we got to the middle of the bridge – though it was wide enough to take a car it was normally closed to traffic – we stopped and looked upstream. The lamps picked out the ripples in the black water below, while high above, a little way upstream, the floodlit west front of the cathedral rose majestically among the trees. 'Nice,' said Mo. At that moment I felt his hand on my shoulder. It wasn't the shoulder next to which he was standing; it was the shoulder on my other side.

I was shocked for a second, but for no longer than that. Once that second was finished I copied his gesture at once. Then... Did I move my head? Did he move his? Did we both do it at the same time? The sides of our heads were touching. Our cheeks brushed each other's, and we felt the static, heard the crackle, of each other's hair.

The bridge and its approaches had been un-peopled till then, but now we heard a voice: someone was walking towards us among the trees. We moved our heads apart, dropped hands from shoulders, then walked on. Neither said a word.

We didn't kiss each other goodnight when we parted on Palace Green. (I had a room in the castle itself, Mo in a modern accommodation block nearby.) That was not, by the way, the night of my most recent hug with Mo. We didn't actually get as far as a hug that night, though there had been several in the year that followed. But it was Mo that I thought of after that first hug from Dickon in Moscow, and remembering the times that Mo and I actually had hugged each other, I was able to drift off to sleep comparing the two experiences in a spirit of wonder, delight and awe.

****

At breakfast the next morning, the morning after my hug with Dickon, one of the other guys in our party called Doctor Cotton by his first name, which was David. The young guy was a student at Aberystwyth; having never seen Doctor Cotton lecturing in bow tie and watch-chain he lacked the preconceptions of him that we Durham folk had. Suddenly we all followed suit. Doctor Cotton became David, losing about ten years in age and a stone in weight in the process, and Doctor Peters became Michael. They joined our group and became human. So did the two dons from York. And

Jenny and a girl friend of hers joined Dickon and me at our breakfast table.

We were out in the bus again, Natasha guiding us, in next to no time. Jenny made a point of sitting next to Dickon, and I got her friend Teresa, who I already knew from my history group at Durham. I liked her, she was very nice, but no substitute for Dickon. However, this morning we weren't travelling far.

It was still snowing, though more lightly than last night, and where it lay it was eighteen inches deep. But already the snow ploughs were busy clearing it, and mobile elevators were lifting it, like huge white loaves of bread into open-topped lorries. 'Where do they go with it?' someone asked, but no-one answered. The bus took us back to Red Square and we had another walk around it. The patches of snow that were out of reach of the snow ploughs were being tackled by shawl-wrapped women with wooden boards on long handles – they looked like estate agents' boards and were deployed like shovels. Michael (who had previously been Doctor Peters) spotted one old woman struggling with a particularly hard patch of compressed ice. He went over to her, borrowed her board and helped her deal with it. None of the rest of us would have done that, but he did. That was the kind of person he was.

The traffic policemen were transformed this morning by their snow-time uniforms of long dark capes and tall pointed hoods. They now looked curiously like monks.

We saw how the lorry-loads of snow were disposed

of. The lorries backed up to the parapet on the edge of the Moskva river and tipped their loads onto its frozen surface. The spring thaw would eventually clear it away.

Little boys swarmed round us. They practised their English. They knew two words of English (just one if you prefer it with a hyphen). The word was chewing-gum. The old Moscow hands among us, the two dons from York, kept a supply for just such eventualities. They distributed their stock and the kids went away happy. Then we got back onto the bus and drove round the corner into the Kremlin.

I had lazily imagined that the Kremlin was a building. Of course it isn't. We found ourselves inside a walled city within a city. Heavily guarded by soldiers, and consisting of small streets and squares on which stood government buildings – ministries, the Palace of Congress – as well a number of cathedrals and monasteries, it had qualities I hadn't expected. Much of it was intriguingly ancient. And, especially with the snow lying thick beside its walkways and on its rooftops, it was beautiful.

We saw the insides of two cathedrals, one dedicated to the Archangel Gabriel, the other to the Annunciation. Russian cathedrals aren't like Western ones with huge naves and transepts. Inside they are warrens of chambers, dark and lamp-lit, filled with gilded icons that glow like jewels. They are also ... cosy. And you get more than one, sometimes, per town.

Natasha showed us the tombs – surprisingly simply

stone slabs marked them – of the Tsars. The line went back for centuries, but at the nearer end it stopped abruptly with Alexander III. I heard Dickon pipe up: 'Where is Nicholas the Second?'

Natasha looked discomfited. 'He isn't here because...' She faltered. 'Because he isn't. Nobody knows where his remains are.' Somebody came to Natasha's aid by asking another, less controversial, question. David walked over to Dickon. For a moment he reverted to being Doctor Cotton. 'Why did you ask Natasha that?' he asked him. 'There was no need to upset Natasha. You knew the answer.' He smiled at Dickon gently. 'Now don't be fractious.'

Dickon didn't answer, but I saw a blush shine dimly through the olive complexion of his cheeks. I too thought Dickon had been unnecessarily provocative. It was hardly Natasha's fault that Nicholas II had been murdered. I would have considered it disloyal of me to criticise Dick, though. But a sudden flash of insight told me that David had taken him to task because he cared not only about Natasha but also about Dickon, and I realised in that moment that there were different ways of showing someone that you cared about them.

We saw the Palace of Congress from the outside. We already knew we would be seeing the inside later in the day. For the building doubled as the Kremlin Opera House in the evenings and our little group had been provided with tickets for tonight. For now, though, there came the Palace of the Metropolitan of Moscow – his was roughly the same job as the Archbishop of

Canterbury's in England – and a magnificent display of church plate and silverware that went back centuries.

'How did all this escape the Revolution?' I found myself asking aloud to anyone who might be standing next to me. It turned out to be my history tutor David.

'The Party tried to suppress the Church completely,' David told me. 'But it found it couldn't. In time it compromised with it, found it a useful ally in controlling the masses. During the Second World War Stalin brought it onside to help maintain the morale of the people. Since then it's stayed in semi-favour, like a dog that lives outside in a kennel.' It seemed funny to hear the name of Stalin on David's lips. Partly because he was a medieval specialist; he didn't teach twentieth-century history. But also because we students had used to say that, with his bristling moustache and determined jaw, he looked a bit like Stalin. Funnily though, this morning, since he'd metamorphosed from Doctor Cotton to David, he seemed less like the dictator than he usually did. 'Some ideas, some ideals, seem to thrive on hardship and difficult times,' I heard him saying. 'God might be one example.' He turned towards me. 'Human love might be another.' The look he gave me was both amused and penetrating. Then he walked off to where another member of our party was beckoning him towards an exhibit. No doubt wanting to ask him another question. Or perhaps the same question. I wondered if he would give the same answer. Love. It wasn't a word I'd been thinking about much. At least, not consciously.

****

It hadn't been love with Mo. At least I didn't think it had been. I was a bit slow to develop perhaps, and at eighteen I had probably been – by a very short whisker – just too young for love. But there had been sex. And I wasn't too young for that.

Sex with Mo had not begun immediately. Not in the days and weeks that followed our walk back from the women's colleges together and that brush of faces and our mutual shoulder clasp while leaning over the parapet of Prebends' Bridge. We continued to talk in the street, or at table if we found ourselves neighbours at mealtimes, but we never referred to what had happened between us; nor did we behave any differently from before. It was as though it had never happened. It was easier that way.

The term ended, the vacation intervened, the summer term began. One evening I was with a group of friends in the bar at the Three Tuns. By chance a neighbouring table was occupied by Mo and a group of his friends. We all knew one another at least a little – we all belonged, after all, to a college consisting of no more than three hundred souls – and so after a while we moved our two tables together, despite the barman's protests, and became one group of about eight. I found myself sitting next to Mo.

Because of the cramped situation it was not surprising

that I sometimes felt the accidental pressure of Mo's knee against my own, out of sight beneath the table top. I was more surprised when I felt a hand alight on that same knee. I did a nano-second's calculation. Yes, it could only be Mo's hand that was contacting me in this way. I turned and looked at him. He looked at me. He didn't move his hand away. Instead he smiled, half shyly, half naughtily. I smiled back at him. Probably in the same mixed way.

After that Mo did remove his hand from my knee; he needed it to lift his pint glass with after all. But our knees remained pressed together for most of the time we remained in the bar. When we'd drunk enough, or had run out of cash, whichever happened first, we rambled back through the streets, upward towards our college. We split off gradually as we passed the various college accommodation blocks and houses. Only I out of this party of eight people lived in the castle building itself. I took advantage of this circumstance. I said to Mo, choosing the moment with split-second timing, just at the parting of our ways, 'Want to come up for a coffee?' I made sure the invitation was directed at him and could not be misconstrued as a general one. It was unusually bold of me, but then I had just had three pints of bitter in the Three Tuns.

'Sure,' Mo said without a beat of hesitation. 'Let's do that.' We parted from the others with nonchalant goodnights and no attempt at subterfuge. We were going off together, just the two of us, for coffee in my room. It was a normal enough thing for university students to do.

I lived in the part of the castle called the keep. It was the highest rampart of the building, rambling up the side of an ancient earthwork about fifty feet high and crowning its summit. 'My God, you've got some steps,' Mo said as we tackled the way up to my room.

'Eighty-nine,' I said with the authority of one who climbed them several times a day. Inside my small room, 'You don't really want coffee, do you?' I said.

'No,' said Mo very matter-of-factly, and the next moment we were in each other's arms.

FOUR

We undressed each other quickly, Mo and I, in a very businesslike way. We were about the same size and build. Even our stiff dicks matched size-wise, though mine was circumcised and his was not. Within moments we were rolling naked on my single bed and trying not to fall off the top. I liked the feel of him; I liked his smell.

We rubbed our cocks against each other's bellies. We kissed each other at the same time; though this seemed to be a matter of form, something we did almost for politeness's sake: it was our bursting cocks that we were really interested in. After a while the mutual rubbing of them against each other's tummies grew too tantalising, too overwhelming to bear and we set about each other's with our hands. In very little time we'd both come, exuberantly jetting fountains over each other and the duvet on the bed. Then we relaxed and held each other, embracing in the complicity of our wetness. For a while it seemed as though we would lie like that, naked and slowly drying on top of the bed for the rest of the night, and that that would be a very nice thing.

It seldom goes quite like that. Eventually we disentangled ourselves gently. Mo fished in his trouser pocket for cigarettes. He offered me one and, though I smoked only rarely, I smoked one with him for companionship's sake. It was as though we were putting a seal on the new development in our friendship. Sitting alongside, naked together, on the side of the bed.

Mo said, 'Do you often do this? I mean, end up with a bloke?'

'Not often,' I admitted. 'Two or three times with guys I was at school with…'

'Same with me,' Mo said. 'Though I'm into girls too, of course.'

'Me too,' I said, although I thought I probably wasn't.

'Better go, I guess,' Mo said when we'd finished our cigarettes. I didn't try to persuade him otherwise. Descending the stairs together at breakfast time, along with the thirty other guys who lived in the keep… We weren't up for that.

We parted with a friendly kiss. And hug. I found myself feeling quite calm as I lay in bed after he'd gone. My thoughts weren't full of dismay or alarm. I wondered whether Mo and I would ever repeat that night's experiment. I found I rather hoped we would. In my mind I ran over the intimate details of what had taken place; I brought back to mind – like Proust – the touches, the sounds, the sights, the smells of the experience. I checked them out. They were all nice. I felt something for Mo that gave me pleasure. It was friendship. It was affection. I asked myself: could it be love? No, was my answer to myself. It wasn't love. Not even the beginning of love. I was quite comfortable with my answer. I didn't have a problem with it.

****

We were getting used to our Moscow hotel, getting used to the idea that we might be given an identical meal at midday and in the evening. Accepting it with the enduring fatalism that we saw everywhere around us. Each main meal began with soup, for which we stood in line like Oliver Twist in the workhouse. The wide soup plates were filled commendably full, though. And they were commendably hot. So hot that you had to hold the rim of the plate with thumbs and forefinger-tips in order to avoid burning your fingers. But that wasn't the end of it. Next to the woman who'd ladled the soup out stood another woman who would plop a large square lump of meat into it as a coup de théâtre. This had the effect of raising the level of the liquid still further till it reached the very edge of the rim of the soup plate and left your thumbs to poach in it. I don't know if the ladle-ladies watched from behind as we struggled to carry our overflowing dishes back to the table.

That afternoon we were taken to the nearby Exhibition Park of National Achievement. We could have walked the one-mile distance but then there would have been nothing to occupy our bus driver. So we went on the bus with Natasha. Again Dickon sat beside Jenny, while I made do with her friend Teresa.

The Exhibition was monumentally dull. The snow in

the park was turning to slush now, as it had stopped falling and the day had warmed considerably. Walking round the park would have been a bore but for the cheering fact that I found myself once again with Dickon. Walking alongside him rather than any of the others made everything seem better. *'Dans le vieux parc, solitaire et glace,'* Dickon suddenly quoted, *'Deux formes ont tout a l'heure passé.'*

'Verlaine,' I said, to show I recognised it. In the old park, alone and frozen, Two figures have just gone past. It was from a terribly sad poem about the failure of love. Verlaine was probably thinking about the end of his relationship with his male lover Rimbaud. I recited the second stanza. *'Leurs yeux sont morts et leurs lèvres sont molles, Et l'on entend à peine leurs paroles.'* Their eyes are dead and their lips are rotten, You can hardly hear their words.

Dickon looked at me. 'Well, that doesn't apply to us,' he said brightly. 'Your lips and eyes look OK to me, and I hear you perfectly.'

'You look all right yourself,' I said, my feelings confused suddenly. 'And I hear you loud and clear.'

Loud and clear in the physical sense only, though. I still didn't know what to make of Dickon. Or of his interest in me. His interest in Jenny.

The only thing in the exhibition that was remotely exciting was a cinema in the round, in which you stood on the floor in the middle while multiple joined-up screens around you played footage filmed from a helicopter. As we dived low over pine forests and swooped up over hillsides it was difficult to stay standing. At one moment Dickon and I found ourselves clutching each other in order to keep our balance. At least I think that was why we clutched each other.

We were back at the Kremlin in the evening. The Palace of Congress made a gynormous opera house. We saw, we heard, Verdi's Don Carlos. I hardly noticed the entrance of the first singer until he opened his mouth. Walking out from behind the open curtain he looked about the size of an ant. In the interval long tables were set out in a vast ante-room, with white cloths on them, and rows of shining glasses on them. Six thousand people were there that night, somebody said. Who were these people? we wondered. These thousands who had turned out for Verdi on a snowy night. All these men dressed in their smart suits and immaculate white shirts that were buttoned up to the top and unadorned with ties. Dickon and Jenny and I could only guess. The great and the good from the various echelons of the Party, we supposed. And the managers of factories who'd reached their production targets. The shop-floor workers who had exceeded theirs. These were the ways – opera tickets, tickets for ice-hockey matches and other sporting events – in which Communist Russia delivered its rewards for being productive, being good.

In the bus back Dickon pointed out the lemon-sellers' kiosks that stood in various places around the town. They were like small newsagents' or tobacconists' kiosks but had only one kind of item for sale. Bright lemons were stacked high in the windows that encircled the solitary seller inside each one. Against the grey, against the snow, against the night they shone like lamps. The streets of Moscow were awash with lemons, it seemed. Their availability was limitless. And yet we never saw anyone approach a kiosk to buy one. There had been none at our hotel. For three days now our glasses of hot tea had been milk-less and lemon-free. Did these wonder fruits that no-one was buying have a price-tag that put them out of the People's reach?

Dickon quoted approximately that great tenet of Communism: 'From each according to his ability to each according to his needs.' He added, 'The trouble is that there's a mis-match. Demand and supply don't seem to meet.'

'Because of unrealistic pricing?' I suggested. I was no economist, but I wanted Dickon to think that I could at least keep up.

There was no goodnight hug between Dickon and me when we'd got undressed for bed that night. David and Michael were in the room with us, and they weren't going to exchange a hug. I went to bed quite happily, though. We'd said our goodnights from under our separate sheets and blankets. In the hearing of the others Dickon had called me Oli and I'd called him Dick. The melodies from Don Carlos were making sleep-inducing patterns in my brain.

****

Mo and I went to bed together three more times in the course of that summer term. My first summer term at Durham. Up to now my only summer term at Durham. Sometimes in my room, sometimes in his room in the accommodation building called Bailey Court. There especially when neither of us felt we could bother with my eighty-nine steps. Each time we masturbated each other to orgasm with huge enthusiasm and enjoyment. We grew relaxed and comfortable with each other as time passed. Comfortable with each other's bodies. Smiling indulgently if the other unloaded too soon. It didn't matter; there was no awkwardness; we were friends; we liked each other's weaknesses and failings as much as we admired each other's strengths. And good looks too, of course. That helped.

The development of our relationship was halted by the summer vacation. But normal service was resumed soon afterwards. We didn't sleep together all the way through till breakfast time, obviously: we still had our student-cred to protect. Our chances with the ladies would be damaged too greatly if the interesting news that we had sex together were to get out. Neither of us needed to say this: it was only too obvious. And yet, little by little, I couldn't help noticing that our post-orgasmic cuddles were increasing in length. And in niceness. Our kisses grew longer and more exploratory. Our hugs too. We never attempted any anal intimacy. We didn't need to voice the shared thought: that outright buggery might be just a little bit too gay for us.

Then Christmas came, and Christmas went. Then began the term that just ten days ago had finished. Mo and I went back to business as usual. But one night, just a few weeks before I set off for Russia, we were sitting naked on the side of Mo's bed and sharing a cigarette – it was the last one in his packet, that's why we were sharing it – and Mo said, 'I'm not sure we should be going on with this.'

It was as though a lift I'd been riding in had snapped its cables all at once. 'Why?' I asked. I was hurtling to the ground without a brake or safety net.

'It's going to make it difficult for us with girls, don't you think?' Mo said. I looked sideways at him but his gaze was fixed on the wall opposite. 'I mean, if we get too used to this… If we get to like it too much…'

If we get to like each other too much, I thought, but didn't come out with it. Personally I didn't care if having sex and being intimate with Mo made it difficult for me to have relationships with girls. I'd rather have had handsome, chunky, blond-furred Mo than any number of girls in my bed. It might be different for him though. I had to accept that. 'If you say so,' I said.

Then Mo slowly got dressed. We hugged goodnight. We even kissed, though it was a careful, thoughtful kiss.

We didn't have sex together again. We met by chance, we chatted in the street. But we did have one last hug. As the vacation came close, 'I'm going on this history department trip to Russia,' I told Mo when we met on the corner of Old and New Elvet.

'Brill,' he said, and his face lit up with a mixture of pleasure that I was going to have an interesting experience, and envy. And a little disappointment, I think, that he wasn't going to have the same experience himself. I didn't go as far as to imagine he wished he was coming with me. All the same he did throw his arms around me on that very public street corner. I threw mine around him. We hugged, though without kissing, for quite a protracted few seconds, taking no notice of the people who came and went. I experienced every instant of that hug most vividly, knowing that I would have to carry it for a long time in my memory, the way a camel carries water through the desert in its stomach. And I'd been right to do so. That was the last hug I'd had, except for my mother's when I parted from her to catch the train to the airport, until the spontaneous embrace I'd shared with Dickon the other night.

****

We had another day and a half in Moscow before heading to our next destinations further east. We spent the first one visiting a place in Moscow's outer suburbs called Zagorsk. This turned out to be a religious centre, a place to which tourists were taken to demonstrate that the church was not persecuted in Russia but allowed to thrive. And in Zagorsk at least, we had to admit, it was thriving heartily. Inside one of the town's many churches we found a wonderful candle-lit central space, with silver canopies and candelabra, full of shrivelled old ladies in black who were repeatedly kissing the venerable icons and singing, in almost unearthly tones, a continuous chant. The sound plucked at my heart. I looked at Dickon's face, over which shadows fluttered in the flickering candle-light, and wondered about his heart.

Apparently the old ladies sang all day in relays, sitting, kneeling, standing, or prostrate in front of one of the icons, forever crossing themselves – then sitting for a while at the back, refreshing themselves with tea and sandwiches before beginning again.

We saw more old ladies, and some younger ones, on the drive back, along the pot-holed but almost traffic-free road into Moscow. These were standing in a freezing river that our bus crossed, and they were doing their washing, shoving it with long poles against the rocks in back-breaking companionship, the way women had done for centuries. And it was a Monday of course... Dickon broke in on my thoughts. But his were the same as mine were. 'Within twelve miles of the Kremlin,' he said.

'What did you think of the chanting?' I asked him.

'That was a bit special, wasn't it?' Again I heard that diffidence in his voice; the hope that I felt the same about it, the insecurity over the possibility that I did not.

'It certainly was,' I said. I wanted to give his hand a squeeze, or better still his cock, but obviously I could not.

By the time we got back for lunch it was four o'clock. But the day wasn't over when we finished it. We went downtown in the light early evening and explored Russia's most famous department store, GUM, in Red Square. Natasha had optimistically compared it to Harrods and Selfridges, neither of which she'd seen. The reality was more like a vast covered market hall, around which sparrows flew and cheeped. Imposing tables were laid out, yet covered with pathetically few goods, and lacklustre ones at that. Michael bought a tube of toothpaste, to prove to himself and the world that one actually could. Dickon observed, 'At least the sparrows are going cheep.' The others groaned. I clasped his awful joke, like a rose, to my heart.

We had also hoped to see the inside of St Basil's while we were in the Square. But for the second day running it was closed to the public.

In the morning, though, we did the tour of Lenin's tomb. Cameras were confiscated at the top of the steps that led down into the mausoleum, but were returned afterwards as we made our way back up. Lenin looked decidedly jaundiced, lying in his glass case, but he was recognisably himself. We'd been privileged. Natasha had led us to the front of the queue for our visit. The queue snaked its way out of Red Square, around the corner and out of sight. Between us all we invented the idea that it stretched all the   way to Vladivostok.

That afternoon we left Moscow, by train from the Kazan station. We were going east, though not as far as Vladivostok. We were going to Vladimir instead.

FIVE

Vladimir had been a capital of old Russia nearly a thousand years ago. A hundred miles east of Moscow it took over two hours to reach, through pine forests and across flat un-hedged wastes of slush and melt-water that probably hid farmland, in a huge train that clucked along at about forty miles per hour. The ancient town that we eventually drew into was a site of international historic importance, mainly on account of its glorious cathedrals and palaces. We would be touring those the next day. For this evening its glory would lie in the meal we got.

We'd grown used to the school-like cafeteria fare in our Moscow hotel. Unexplainable cuts of meat, or else frankfurters, accompanied by noodles or starchy grains that were made to seem like rice, the way coal dust can be compressed into ovoid nuts. There would have been soup with its cube of meat splashed into it like a boulder at the last moment, and Russian salads – which admittedly were quite nice. No dessert except a repetitive sticky bun. But now, this evening, in a hotel in Vladimir, we dined at tables with white tablecloths, in an elegant pilastered dining room, on steak and chips. Not horse but real beef steak. And real chips. Russian salad, and gherkins the size of men's cocks. (Those slipped down a treat.) The atmosphere was festive, celebratory.

But this wasn't to be our billet for the night. We would be sleeping for the next two nights in a small hotel in the next town, the beautiful smaller city of

Suzdal, twenty miles away. Suzdal had been the Russian capital even before Vladimir. We set off there, in the luminous evening dark, by bus.

It was a new experience for me to leave one small town by night and to see the lights of the next one, our destination, shimmering in the distance, twenty miles across the flat, flat plain, with not a single other light between. It was more like crossing the sea and seeing your port of arrival twenty miles away across the water. And it took about the same length of time to make the crossing. Our bus jogged along among the pot-holes at about the speed of a Channel ferry.

Suzdal was small, beautiful and remote. We walked around its quiet streets before bed. Snow fell lightly upon and around us. We paused in front of a snow-white monastery and heard the night wind hum softly among its cupolas. The cupolas were dark blue, with gold stars embossed all over them, so that they seemed to form a mirror of the star-studded dome of the heavens above.

We stood on the old ramparts and looked back to where the lights of Vladimir glowed comfortingly twenty miles away across the flat dark waste. 'We're standing where the Princes of Suzdal stood,' said a voice in my ear. It was Dickon's voice of course. 'Looking fearfully across the endless flatness to the lands from which the Mongol hordes might come at any moment...'

I said, 'Do you think they'll come tonight?' I was happy. Not only because I had come to a wonderfully beautiful and deeply moving place. We had sorted out our hotel rooms when we'd arrived. Our group filled the small hotel. We were all in twin rooms this time. I had made sure ... and I thought Dickon had also been aiming for this ... that we would be roommates for the coming two nights.

We didn't quite face each other as we undressed. But neither did we turn our backs. We saw enough of each other's nakedness to form an opinion before we got into bed. Dickon had a lovely lean physique. His limbs and chest were smooth, olive-skinned and nearly hairless. His raven dark hair grew thickly only on his head, beneath his armpits and around his cock. His legs were long and so was his dick. Dick's dick. It hung thick and heavy between his thighs; it was circumcised, like mine, and had a handsome plum-dark head. What Dickon made of my own adornment and of my physique in general I couldn't tell, though I could see him looking at my body while I was looking at his. There wasn't much to be done, though; no point worrying about it. I knew my cock was on the big side for a lad of my size, while, as for my scrawny body, it was the only one I had.

There is something special about chatting with a friend when you are in twin beds in the same room and the lights are out. Even when there is nothing sexual about the conversation or the ambient static. We discover this as kids and adolescents. Perhaps it happens less in adult life, but I wouldn't know that yet. At any rate there was a very lovely atmosphere surrounding my after-lights-out conversation with Dick that night. We turned ourselves inside out. We revealed our hopes and fears, acknowledged our failings and weaknesses. Then at last Dickon brought the subject up. 'Are you gay, Oli?' he asked.

'No,' I said.

'Nor me,' said Dickon. 'I mean, some of my friends are, but I'm not.'

'It's the same with me,' I said. Oh shit, I thought.

I hadn't yet admitted to myself that I was homosexual. I certainly hadn't told anybody else that I was. I wasn't ready to tell Dickon I was gay; that would have meant confronting the awkward fact myself. All the same, I was well aware that I had probably just lied to my lovely roommate. I realised that out of fear I had shut the door on who knew what realm of possibility, delight and ... I tried not to think the word ... love. What didn't cross my mind for even a second was that Dickon might have just lied to me, and to himself, in an identical act of cowardice.

The atmosphere of trust and friendship that had been building between us – it seemed as three-dimensional and as wonderful as one of the white and gold cathedrals we were getting used to seeing around us – now dissipated. *Like the baseless fabric of this vision, melted into air, into thin air...* We found we had nothing more to say to each other. At least, there was nothing more to be said tonight. Just our civil departure from the day just ended, and from each other. 'Well, sleep tight, Oli,'

Dickon said.

'Sleep tight, Dick,' I said. 'Goodnight.' I could hardly get the words out. My bitter disappointment with the way things had just ended, my bitter self-reproach for my cowardice, choked my throat and stung my eyes and cheeks. Had I been alone I might have broken down and sobbed. But I wasn't alone and I didn't allow myself that. Dickon would have heard me and wondered what on earth… Again, it never even occurred to me that Dickon, silent in his bedtime darkness, might be undergoing the same pain that I was in; that he might be in the same state.

The luxury of breakfast in Suzdal! A sunlit dining room, fresh snow outside, fresh bread within, and individual soufflés in earthenware pots with miniature sausages buried in them – a sort of vertical toad-in-the-hole. Then back in the bus and over the pot-holed road to Vladimir at a jog-trot. Our first engagement, a bit perversely in this city of history and beauty, was a tour of a tractor factory – a tractory factory as Natasha repeatedly and delightfully called it. We were escorted round the premises by the factory managers, all dressed in their smart suits and immaculate white shirts that were buttoned up to the top and unadorned with ties.

But things got progressively better after that. A tour of the town museum was followed by visits to the carved white stone church of Dmitriev and the gilt-domed cathedral of the Assumption, full of frescoes of talismanic power.

Lunch, again in individual pots, was what is known in Britain as Lancashire hotpot, and was just as good. After lunch we toured Vladimir's twelfth-century Golden Gate, and (in an odd juxtaposition) a teacher training college, which Natasha referred to each time, not without difficulty, as a pedagogical institute. Later, a dance band played in our grand restaurant while we ate dinner, and then it was back on the bus across the snow to where the golden lights of Suzdal beckoned us from the distance. I didn't spend much time with Dickon that day. I sat with Jenny both ways on the bus. In the light of my conversation with Dickon the previous night, and of what Mo had said just a few weeks ago about having sex with guys making it difficult to feel the same about women, I wondered if I ought to try and have sex with Jenny but the idea of it didn't sit easily in my mind. It just didn't feel right.

Everyone admitted to feeling tired when we got back to our little hotel in Suzdal. Everyone began to drift off to their rooms for the night. Dickon and I found ourselves together at the foot of the stairs, ready to take the first upward step. But just before either of us made that move Dickon turned and looked at me. He had that shy, diffident look in his face that always came over it when he was going to suggest something I might not go along with. 'Want to go for a walk?' The shy diffidence had also stolen into his voice.

'Yes,' I said simply. Dickon might not be gay but still I would have walked anywhere with him. Back to

Vladimir through the snow if necessary. Maybe to Vladivostok.

'Round the ramparts?' Dickon said.

I remembered how magical the ramparts had looked last night. 'Neat,' I said.

The streets were empty of people, carpeted with fresh snow which lay partially in darkness and partially sparkling in the throw of the street-lamps. Dickon and I moved, every thirty yards, from light to darkness as we walked and then back into crisp gold light. We hardly spoke; it didn't seem the moment for that.

The ramparts were a raised earthwork that surrounded the town. The town was entirely contained within them, a huddle of roofs, of cathedral and monastery walls and floodlit onion domes. On the outside the earth wall, steep as a railway embankment, fell away into a darkness that stretched away in all directions like an ocean. Only the lights of Vladimir, distantly shimmering, provided a reference point, like a homing beacon, exactly in the south. The wind had blown the snow clouds away a night ago and they hadn't come back. The sky was clear and cold, the stars shone like snow crystals and the moon sat among them, a slender crescent of silver ice.

We could follow the gradually curving line of the rampart easily enough. Beneath the snow on its top was probably a public path. As we walked its long circuit the white towers and glittering cupolas inside the town appeared to revolve with us, like fancy goods in a shop-window display case. We got about halfway round the circle, but then the way in front of us was blocked by a fence. We stopped and inspected it.

'It's only a garden fence,' said Dickon. That was true. It wasn't high and we could see the garden on the other side of it. We could see the fence on the other side of the garden, and that wasn't high either. We stood stock still and listened. There were cold rustles of breeze occasionally but apart from that there was nothing but silence. We looked at each other. 'Go for it?' Dickon queried.

'Why not?' I said.

It wasn't that difficult to scramble up and over the fence. The difficulty was to do it without breaking the flimsy structure of larch-lap panels as we went. But by balancing ourselves carefully as we went over, and each holding the panel steady while the other climbed it we managed to do just that.

We'd got halfway across the garden when the dog woke up. One moment it was just a nearby bark, the next we could hear it rushing towards us across the snow from the direction of the house. There was just enough light from the moon for us to see its movement but not enough to show us what kind of dog it was, or how big.

I'd never done the hurdle sprint at school; I'd never thought I'd be any good at it; but I'd been wrong about that. I was over the next fence as fast as any Olympic champion, Dickon alongside me, part scrambling, part vaulting, landing at the end of a flying leap. We crossed the next garden in about a second and vaulted the next fence. By now there were dogs barking from kennels outside every house. Bedroom lights were coming on as householders were woken by the racket.

Garden succeeded garden and fence followed fence. Every fence was made of larch-lap – which by some miracle we never broke – and every garden contained a dog. I felt one brush my leg with its muzzle and I kicked out at it as I leaped for the next barrier of larch-lap.

The sequence seemed never-ending. Garden after garden, dog after dog, fence after fence. When we reckoned up afterwards we made it come to a total of about four but while we were going through them it felt more like twenty. But at last we cleared a fence that didn't bring us into another garden. We hardly dared to believe our eyes as we saw the public rampart walk resume its unimpeded progress ahead of us. But we stopped for no more than half a second. I said, 'Keep running for a bit.' The words were hardly necessary. We were already sprinting ahead, putting as much distance as we could, and quickly, from the rumpus behind us and from the bedroom lights.

Somehow we could hear that, apart from the scrunch of our own flying footsteps, no sound was following; that the barking of dogs was growing faint behind us. As if a single thought dictated the actions of both of us we abruptly came to a stop at the same precise instant.

And grabbed each other.

'Are you all right?'

'I'm OK. I was afraid for you.'

'I was frightened for you. I'm OK.'

We'd been frightened for ourselves too but there was no need to say that. We stood wrapped in each other's arms. We could feel each other trembling through our thick winter coats. After the first second or two of mutual reassurance we could have let each other go: the initial shock had gone. But a new shock had replaced it: the shock of our embrace. The power of it. The thirsty need.

Dick's arms were round me; I felt them as intensely as if they'd been bare and were touching my naked skin. The feeling of them was imprinting itself on my mind like mental fingerprints. Handprints. Wristprints. Forearm-prints. Biceps-prints. With my own fingers I counted his vertebrae and gouged between his bones. His ribs; the iliac crests of his pelvis. I felt Dick's leather-gloved hands move: one upward, one downward. With the one he embraced my neck and then began to rub the back of my head through my hair. With the other he cupped, one after the other, the small domes of my buttocks, then he pressed the blade of his hand in between.

I kissed him then. He let me do it on his lips. Then he kissed me in return. How is it that even when one person is three inches taller than another their lips always manage to meet with ease when they kiss?

It seemed that we were both too overcome with the wonder, the unexpectedness of it to find the presence of mind to stop. But there was nobody about on the breezy ramparts. There was no-one to see us. No-one nearer than the inhabitants of Vladimir, the town whose lights twinkled at us across the snow from twenty miles away. There was no obvious reason why our kiss should ever end.

Though it did, of course, as all kisses do. You get hungry; you get cramp; you get cold; you need to breathe. In our case, with the wind coming at us from the Ural mountains six hundred miles away across the flatlands, it was mainly the cold.

'Shall we continue our circuit?' Dick asked as soon as his mouth was free.

'May as well,' I said. 'We've almost come full circle.' Sometimes you find you've accidentally said something that is true in more ways than you thought.

SIX

We nodded to the receptionist as we walked through the half-lit entrance hall. Apart from that solitary figure behind the desk there was no sign of anybody else. The rest of our party seemed all to have gone to bed. Inspired by their example we climbed the stairs. Not till we were inside our room with the door shut behind us did we wrap ourselves around each other again.

Then we took each other's gloves off, released each other from those winter coats. I pulled Dick's pullover off over his head and he did the same with mine. There were warm cowboy type shirts to deal with next, then vests. By unspoken agreement we dealt with our own shoes and socks, but then we returned to each other to fumble with belts and flies of jeans.

We grew impatient then. Didn't pull each other's jeans right off but immediately went on to release each other's erect and bouncy cocks from the underpants that were doing little to conceal them anyway. Then, with pants and jeans still snagged halfway down our thighs we pressed ourselves hard into each other, mashing our dicks against each other's bellies, hot and hard.

As we kissed I felt Dick's middle finger steal downward between my buttock cheeks and explore the contours of the tight and tiny knot of muscle that guarded my arsehole. Nobody had ever done this to me before. With an unexpected tingle of excitement I realised that I wanted him to put his finger right inside. He didn't. But with my feelings caught off guard I found myself suddenly doing exactly that to him.

'Ow,' he said, and his whole body tensed with his surprise.

'Sorry,' I said, and took my finger out like a wine bottle cork.

'Ow,' he said again. Then he chuckled as he hugged me reassuringly. 'It's OK,' he said. 'I like it really. But it's better if you wet your finger first. Spit or something.'

'Sorry,' I said again.

'Don't be,' Dickon said, grinning between kisses. 'Shall we have a shower?'

'Together?' I asked. Unlike the room we'd shared with David and Michael in Moscow this one in Suzdal had an en suite bathroom with a shower.

'I'd like that,' said Dick. Once again he became sweetly unsure of things as he asked, 'Wouldn't you?'

'Of course,' I said, and yanked his jeans and pants down to his ankles, then off his feet – which he raised helpfully one after the other – to show that I really meant it.

I'd never shared a shower with another guy. I guessed from the confident way that he handled things – I mean the situation as well as my cock and balls – that Dickon already had some experience in this line, but I wasn't going to ask him about it now.

We soaped each other down and washed each other's hair. We washed each other's cocks and balls especially carefully, pretending this devoted attention was a hygienic necessity rather than an erotic pleasure, discovering all those almost invisible creases that even circumcised boys like us harbour behind the glans. Then with sudsy fingers we entered each other's anuses properly and comfortably. Under the nonsensical pretext that we were giving each other a good clean out we pushed our middle fingers all the way in; it felt marvellous both ways round.

I thought we probably wouldn't go quite as far as to fuck each other in the shower. I'd never fucked or been fucked by anybody; I thought it quite probable that Dickon hadn't either; it was another thing I wasn't going to ask him right now. Instead, standing with feet well apart to prevent us falling over, supporting each other by leaning warm belly against warm belly, and each with a finger still inserted in the other's rear end, we started to wank each other's cocks.

No sooner started than we were ready to go. I felt Dickon's legs stiffen and brace at the same moment as I felt mine doing so. I felt the surge of my onrushing orgasm welling through my thighs and stomach and groin; I felt my whole being rising towards release like a captive bird – a swallow or a swift. And I knew from the feel of his cock in my hand, and from the way he looked and the way his body felt in my embrace that the same thing was happening to Dick at the same time.

We hardly saw our semen spurts emerge. The water from the shower was still running down us fast and hot. But we saw that water flash suddenly with white in repeated bursts as we simultaneously came, as if we were washing paintbrushes under a running tap and squeezing them with our fingers to a regular pulse.

The static dissipated. Our muscles relaxed. The water ran clear once more. Painlessly we removed our fingers from each other's orifice and hugged and kissed under the running water one last time. Then, anticlimactically, post-climatically, we turned the water off and stepped out of the shower.

Though of course we had fun towelling each other dry.

We didn't discuss the question of which bed we would sleep in; we just climbed both together into Dickon's and held each other, caressed each other's nakedness, when we got there. We hardly said a word, even when, some twenty minutes later, we brought each other off a second time. Then Dick did say, 'I hadn't come for ages. Haven't had a wank for days.'

'Nor me,' I said. Then we held each other tightly for a second and both giggled. We didn't need to explain the reason why we hadn't been able to wank for days.

I woke up first.

Did I? Doesn't it always seem that we're the first to wake, while the other one sleeps on? Maybe they've woken first, had a look at the sleeping face on the pillow beside them and then drifted off again – contentedly or discontentedly as the case may be.

Anyway, I woke up first that next morning, or at least I thought I did. I spent some time observing the sleeping face beside me, its contours picked out by the lights and shadows of a Russian dawn. I was relieved to discover, on questioning myself carefully, that I liked what I saw.

A minute or two later Dick opened his eyes. He looked into mine for a moment with what might have been puzzlement. He seemed to be seeing me through a veil. And then he smiled. I said, 'Hi. Are you OK?'

'Yes, I'm OK,' he answered quietly. 'Are you?'

'Yes,' I said. Then, 'I meant – are you OK about what happened…? I mean last night…?' I tailed off.

I heard Dick draw in a quick breath of surprise that was both sharp and soft at the same time. I felt his brain was whirling through the events of the last twelve hours – including whatever dreams he'd had while his sleeping body had cuddled me during the last eight of them – and processing everything in computer-quick time. The analysis took just over a second to complete. Then he smiled and said, 'Yes. I'm OK with everything that's happened. With everything we did.' Relief flooded through me as I listened to   that. Especially the last bit.

Without uncoupling from each other we pressed closely into each other's bed-moist warmth and did the last bit again.

This was to be our full day in Suzdal. It was a relaxing feeling: knowing we weren't going to be shepherded anywhere by bus or train. Instead we headed out on foot into the pretty streets as soon as breakfast was over. The wind had dropped during the night but the sky remained clear and blue. The snow still lay fresh and deep; it wasn't thawing yet, but there was a heady spring warmth in the sunny air.

There were thirty-six ancient churches is little old Suzdal. We didn't visit them all, but as they were all crowded into the small centre of the place, within its walls, we managed to see quite a few. First the Rozhdestvensky Cathedral (its English name was just as big a mouthful: Cathedral of the Nativity of the Holy Virgin). It was the one we'd seen from the outside on our first night: the one with the five star-studded blue domes atop its ice-sculpture towers. Its interior was reassuringly gilded and icon-filled. Nearby, across a snow meadow and near a stream stood a small wooden church that had been put together in the seventeenth century without the use of a single nail.

Beside that church, beside the stream, was a line of small trees which Dick and I, full of the exuberance of that spring morning, started to climb, and we were soon pursued up into the branches by the other boys in our group. David and Michael looked up at us, grinning, but declined to join us aloft when Dick laughingly invited them to. The girls on the ground threw snowballs at us and when we'd rejoined them we all joined in with chucking them at the cawing, flapping rooks that were nesting higher up.

I couldn't get enough of that morning. I wanted to hold onto every breath of the wonderful fresh air; I wanted never to let it out again; I wanted it to remain part of me. I wanted to feel the sunshine penetrating my clothes and anointing my skin for ever. I hardly need to add that I wanted Dickon in the same way.

As we walked around the little town (if you took away the thirty-six churches and the old Bishops' Palace it would have amounted to nothing bigger than a village) it seemed that Dick and I were always side by side. The rest of the group changed places with one another as we walked together, chatting now with one, then with another companion. They came and chatted with us, and we went and chatted with them, but there were clearly two of us who were together now. We walked as though an invisible yoke bound us together. As indeed it did. The invisible yoke of sex.

'You're still on speaking terms at least,' Jenny said to us at one moment. We were walking through the 15th-century rooms of the Bishops' Palace. 'Sharing a room together but still friends in the daytime.'

'At least,' I said, letting Jenny make what she would of that. Dick gave a small snort of surprise, or maybe of pleasurable embarrassment. I was letting him make what he would of the remark too.

'See you at lunch,' Jenny said, and smiled. A knowing smile, was it? I wasn't clever enough to read its runes. She dropped back and rejoined Teresa, her own roommate here in Suzdal.

We took a meandering route back to the hotel. It led along back streets that were unpaved lanes that became muddy farmyards that then became lanes again. There were timber cottages with dung heaps beside them. Blue wood-smoke rose lazily from their chimneys and scented the air. Ducks, geese and hens mooched around and splashed in the puddles.

Suddenly we were in the middle of a funeral procession. It travelled on foot, the coffin bearers and the followers all swathed in black. We stopped in our tracks. The coffin passed right beside us. With a shock we saw that it was open-topped. The body of a young woman lay inside. Her face, though pinched by death, looked serene enough. Involuntarily I touched fingers with Dickon, standing at my side. Neither of us was wearing gloves this sunny day. For a second, but for no more than a second, we felt the life-affirming warmth of each other through our finger-ends. We didn't clasp hands. Not then.

It was the first time either of us had seen a corpse, we discovered when we discussed it later. OK, it was the second if you counted the embalmed body of Lenin which we'd seen in his mausoleum beneath Red Square, but this one, the dead remains of that young woman whose life had been cut short by who knew what at an early age, seemed much more real. The procession made its way across the mud and snow towards the nearest of the available churches. Even from where we stood we could see six of those.

Although the afternoon was a 'free' one – no organised trips or walks were planned, and Natasha was taking a well-earned afternoon off – neither Dickon nor I suggested that we should bolt straight up to our bedroom immediately after lunch. It would have made things more blatantly obvious to the rest of the group than any of us would at that time have been comfortable with. Instead we went out for another walk through the countrified little place, just the two of us. The others also went for walks through the town in twos or threes, exploring its hidden corners, and we all crossed paths from time to time on street corners, stopped and chatted and told each other what we'd just seen. And all of it was wonderful and strange; the simplest things no less than the funeral that we'd encountered in the morning were novelties in our Western – and youthful – eyes.

The tiny, placid central square boasted a row of shops that ran along one of its sides. Small shops, and just a few, but shops all the same. In our almost-a-week in Russia we hadn't seen many of those. Dickon and I saw one that in our home country would have been called an off-licence, elsewhere a liquor store. We'd been warned about shops in Moscow. They weren't for the likes of us, apparently. Tourists were encouraged to use the *Berioska* shops which had been set up expressly to bring the hard currencies of the countries from which tourists came into the economy. You didn't spend roubles in the berioska shops but dollars or pounds. We didn't know what would happen to us, or to our roubles, if we went inside a shop such as the one we now stood outside.

Dickon and I looked at each other for a second then, without speaking, immediately plunged inside.

The shop's interior was cramped and dark, yet surprisingly well stocked with booze. No western brands of course. The Martinis, Jack Daniel's, Drambuies and Southern Comforts just weren't there. But there were wines from the Caucusus and from Georgia, and there was vodka in a profusion of different bottles and illegible names. We selected one at random – we liked the label – and took it to the counter apprehensively. Somehow we expected that at any moment some agent of the state would appear from nowhere, confiscate our hoped-to-be trophy (as our cameras had been confiscated at Lenin's tomb) and bundle us out of the shop unceremoniously. Or worse. We might never be seen again.

But there was no problem at all. The shopkeeper wrapped our purchase for us, took a couple of roubles in payment (the price was wondrous low) and then said *Dasvidanya* (au revoir) with a smile. With a smile! That took us aback. In all our days in Moscow we hadn't seen a single smile. It seemed that Russia kept her smiles hidden away here in remote Suzdal.

There was to be a party that night: that we knew. Some of the vodka would be our contribution to the occasion. But in the meantime…

We returned to our hotel an hour or two before dinner. There was nobody from our party to be seen at that moment and we took advantage of this fact to head straight upstairs to our room. There were two clean glasses in the bathroom. Dick fetched them at once, and I unscrewed the top of the bottle. Even before we took our coats off. Even before we kissed.

SEVEN

We only just made it downstairs in time for dinner. It would have looked rather too obvious had we come down actually late. As it was it still looked obvious, but only mildly so.

We hadn't made very serious inroads into the vodka. One generous glass each had warmed us up sufficiently to make us want to take each other's clothes off and get into bed. And what happened there was a very predictable repeat of what we'd already done several times before. But we hadn't yet got blasé about doing that. We were still finding each other's bodies a pair of magical wonderlands, warm and scented, vast as the Russian plains and skies that surrounded us, vaster than we could ever completely explore. Dickon kept his watch on in bed. I'd never met anyone who did that before; it was something that had never occurred to me. I marvelled at the exotic novelty of this; but then everything about Dickon was novel and exotic. In fact it was just as well that he kept his watch on: we probably would have been late for dinner otherwise.

It was our last night in Suzdal and all the stops were pulled out for that final dinner here. We were served a seven-course traditional Russian meal. The first course was the filler – mashed potato swirled into attractive rosette shapes with large gherkins stuck into the mound and dill tendrils for garnish. It served its purpose and looked wonderful, but it tasted of exactly what it was.

Which was mashed potato. The courses that followed were more interesting: much smaller but more refined. Gherkins and tomatoes cooked together slowly with cabbage was the next one. Then mushrooms stewed in yoghurt or sour cream ... which we were learning to call *smetana* (placing the accent on the middle syllable as in Svetlana or sultana). There was steak braised in beer with buckwheat, and then there were pancakes with honey, which we washed down with mead. The final course was a drink. Natasha told us it was a very traditional Russian speciality and was served on special occasions. It turned out to be tea with milk in it, which was a bit of an anticlimax for us Brits. Still, it managed to taste quite unlike any other cup of tea with milk in it that I had ever drunk. Perhaps it was the tea that was different. Perhaps it was the milk.

Scarcely had we finished that final course than our farewell party began. It involved all of us, and Natasha, and – slightly more surprisingly – all the managers from the 'tractory' factory that we had toured the day before in Vladimir. The tractory managers were still in their suits and their white shirts, buttoned up to the collar but without ties. They were armed with bottles of vodka. Some of our party nipped up to their rooms and returned with bottles of whisky that they'd bought in the town that afternoon. Others came down with bottles of vodka. Dickon went up and brought down what was left of ours.

Our new Russian friends, who were exclusively male, turned out to be, now that we were meeting them off duty, full of charm and bonhomie. They were not only very well disposed towards us; they were highly educated and able to talk interestingly about science, history and literature in excellent English. They were enthusiastic about the opportunities for change that were being presented by the new man in the Kremlin, Mr Gorbachev. They all saw him as someone who could unlock a door to a new future that until now had been firmly closed. We visitors from Britain began the evening by being well disposed towards our tractory visitors too. With the ingestion by all of copious quantities of vodka and whisky the mutual respect and appreciation between our two groups only grew.

Some time around midnight the hotel staff told us they were closing the lounge and restaurant areas. We all withdrew upstairs and continued drinking and talking in the big corridor, wide as a cloister, that ran along outside all our rooms. At last, when the bottles were empty and we Brits at any rate were beyond coherent conversation, it became time to say goodnight to our guests. They enveloped us with powerful bear-hugs as they took their leave. I'd never been hugged by so many grown men at one time before. It was rather nice, I thought. My last memory of that party evening was the sight of one of our young lads from York whirling David Cotton up and down the bedroom corridor in a stomping dance. It was a sight that was memorable as well as startling: taking to the dance floor with David was not something that any of us Durham boys would have dreamed of doing, however much the social gap had narrowed between us and our tutor in medieval history.

I awoke with a thundering head and limbs that grieved if I moved them so much as an inch. But that wasn't the worst of it. I was alone in bed. In panic I raised my head from the pillow despite its protests, and was partly relieved to see Dickon fast asleep in his own bed a couple of feet away, his blanket cover partway down and his arms flailed out at the sides. My body wasn't yet up to the task of getting out and going over to shake him. 'Dick,' I called across to him. 'Seven o'clock. Time to get up. Early start.' His shuttered eyes came open stickily, they half-focused on me and then, smiling bleakly, he groaned himself awake.

Neither of us could remember going to bed. Had we collapsed into our separate beds to begin with? Or had we climbed into one bed together then, in the small hours, had one of us half woken and climbed out from our tangled nest of limbs, and for the sake of comfort gone back to his own bed for the remainder of the night? We discussed this question later in puzzlement but we never found out.

We all, all sixteen of us, looked a bit shell-shocked as we struggled with our seven-fifteen breakfast in the lovely old pilastered dining room. That went for David and Michael and the two dons from York as much as it did for us younger folk. But we put a brave face on things – all of us did – and staggered out to the waiting bus. Then it was off across the twenty heaving miles of pot-holes to the station in Vladimir. There … guess what … to our astonishment … there were our party guests from the previous night, lined up in the station car-park, dressed in their smart suits and immaculate white shirts that were buttoned up to the top and unadorned with ties, and they were waving us cheerful, exuberant goodbyes. *Dasvidanya, dasvidanya*, on all sides. Somehow, as well as being surprised, we were all absurdly but genuinely touched. It was clear to me at that moment that Russian men didn't waste time with effete hangovers. It was equally clear, as I looked around me at our suffering group, that we were made of much less sturdy stuff.

We travelled back through the time-warp pine forests, still snow-clad like Narnia, and were back in grey Moscow by the morning's end. Then back to our grim grey hotel in time for a grim grey lunch. At least by that time our hangovers were past their zeniths.

The afternoon was museum time. Natasha, bouncy and energetic as a Russian Tigger, got us onto yet another bus and we did the Pushkin Museum. It was actually an art gallery, magnificent, startlingly well-endowed with Brueghels, Picassos and French Impressionists. I found myself wanting to put my hand into Dickon's as we walked round, but I couldn't. I also wanted to clasp his dick – Dick's dick – as we walked from picture to picture but of course I couldn't do that. Instead we walked round all the exhibits side by side, in pair formation, and that had to be enough. Even doing that made it clear to the others – we could see the realisation on their faces – that something special had happened between the two of us. Even if they weren't sure exactly what that something special was.

76

Back to our hotel for dinner... But we wouldn't be sleeping there tonight. After the meal we piled our luggage into our battle bus and headed straight out again to the Moscow State Circus. Like the opera house we'd been to just a few days earlier it was packed with an audience of thousands. There wasn't an empty seat to be seen in the house. The show was grand and spectacular. Underfunded it was not. It was heavy on clowns – among them the great Popov – and heavy on animals. Lions, tigers, pumas, dogs and bobcats all played their parts. We all loved watching their virtuosic performances (that was clear to me from watching the faces of the others) but then we all said afterwards how deplorable, how demeaning, and how cruel to the animals it was. None of us, evidently, was above being a bit of a hypocrite when the moment demanded it.

By that time we were on board our bus again, weaving our way through the nearly deserted streets to the Leningrad station in order to catch the overnight sleeper train. 'I saw a documentary once,' I told Dick as we sat together on the bus, 'about the Moscow Leningrad railway. It made me interested. It made it seem very...' I couldn't bring myself to use the word. The word was *romantic*, of course. But the word was like an unlighted match in a space full of petrol fumes. I didn't dare strike it. Who knew what would happen to us if I did?

'I think I saw the same one,' I hear Dick say. I felt his long thigh press lightly against mine. 'It was ...' He faltered. Perhaps he had come up against the same incendiary word that I had. '...As you say. Doesn't it run straight as an arrow the whole four hundred miles?'

'Something like that,' I said, and applied the pressure of my own thigh to his in return for his little push. We hadn't had any proper sexual contact, hadn't ejaculated together, for about thirty hours. We were both feeling the strain. We were super-horny for each other and our skins crawled with frustrated desire.

'Make sure we're in the same sleeping-compartment,' said Dickon, reminding himself and stiffening his own resolve as much as telling me to act.

'Sure,' I said. 'It'll probably be a four, but even so. And we must insist on getting a room together in whatever hotel they take us to in Leningrad.'

'That may be fours again too,' said Dick a bit Eeyoreishly.

I said, 'It must be possible to get a two. We can insist on it.' Those were brave words but they must have sounded empty. Insisting on things with Natasha never got anyone very far, as we'd had a week in which to learn, and taking the thing up with hotel staff or management would have been difficult for two guys who hadn't a word of Russian between them except for goodbye, please and thank you.

We came to the station, hauled our luggage down from the racks overhead and headed out of the bus, through the grand ticket hall and towards the train that was waiting for us beyond the concourse.

I'd never been on a sleeper train. I'd seen such things in films. In those an atmosphere of suspense and excitement always attended the scenes of boarding, of pulling out of the platform into the night and accelerating gradually, inexorably, into the unknown beyond. The action that was to come usually involved love or spies. Sometimes both. Now here I was, with Dickon beside me, enacting these scenes for real. I made the happy discovery that it was even better than the films when it came to real life.

As we carried our bags along the endless platform we negotiated with two of the other Durham guys: they were fellow members of my history group and I knew them well. If the compartments turned out to have four bunks apiece as we'd surmised then we four would share. Ahead of us Natasha led the way. She had the tickets, knew which carriage was ours, was in charge.

Natasha came to a halt. She beckoned us like a traffic policeman, waved us in through carriage doors. The compartments were, as we'd expected, made for four. We, Dickon and I and my two Durham friends, piled into one and threw our bags carelessly onto one bunk or other. Nobody cared, let alone discussed, who would have top or bottom bunk, who would sleep above, below or opposite whom. It was hardly going to matter: we'd be using the compartment for a mere eight hours.

It was eleven o'clock but we were all too keyed up and excited to climb into bed and go to sleep right there and then. Freed of our luggage we tumbled back into the corridor and saw that all the rest of our party had had the same thought.

The train was still in the station but doors were being pushed to from the outside with thunderous clangs. The corridor was full of people; it was a long narrow hive of comings and goings. At one end of the carriage was a communal toilet, at the other... I'd never seen anything like this before. An old black-shawled woman sat – I was learning to call these women babushkas – next to a small black charcoal stove. The top part of the stove was formed of a cast-iron mass-catering version of the traditional samovar. Below, the charcoal glowed crimson and sent up unthreatening little scarlet flames. The apparatus, and the babushka, looked older than the train and that itself looked far from new. The people who were lined up in the corridor were already, by force of circumstance, in the ideal configuration to make a queue, and somehow became transformed immediately, without any effort or conscious decision, into exactly that. We found ourselves an integral and un-protesting part of it.

A rumour ran back towards us from the head of the line. 'She's got wine,' the rumour ran. And so it proved. In a cupboard behind her back the old lady guarded bottles of ink-dark red wine. They were screw-topped, we saw when we got closer. That made life easier. We reached in our pockets for roubles, and bought a bottle between us four. There were plastic cups to drink it from. It wasn't half good.

But we didn't want to miss out on the experience of a bedtime glass of black tea with an insoluble cube of sugar in it, dispensed by a babushka from a samovar in a

Russian train. It was an experience that perhaps we would never have again. So we bought one of those each too, holding the wine-cup in one hand and the scalding hot tea-glass in the other as we stood and chatted, high on the novelty of it all, in the crowded corridor.

As we'd queued alongside the big windows, moving slowly up the line our train had done the same. Whistles had blown. The platform staff's, and then the sonorous answering blast from the locomotive at the head of the train. Slowly we'd started to move, the platform sliding alongside us for a time – indeed for so long a time that it seemed the platform would never come to an end but stay with us all the way to Leningrad. But then at last it slipped suddenly away behind us. The station lights were gone and the darkness was pierced only by the pinprick lines of lights from trackside apartment blocks and their long thin reflections among the silver rails.

The Moscow suburbs dragged by for ages. They lasted easily as long as the hot tea and the warming red Georgian wine. But then all was finished. The big windows of the corridor were black and blank, empty of everything save the reflections of our young faces looking out. The same went for our glasses and plastic cups of wine. We handed those back to our babushka (Spassibo) and went back to our compartments, where we pulled our bags off our bunks, groped inside them for pyjamas and toothbrushes, then formed an orderly queue of four at the minute washbasin.

There was no question of any sort of sex between Dickon and me in that confined space shared among four, or of our climbing publicly into the same bunk bed. The bunks were too narrow anyway. It would have been like sleeping together on a windowsill. In any case I went to sleep as soon as my head touched the pillow. I just remember looking up for a second at the underside of the bunk above me, registering the odd but wonderful fact that Dickon was up there, invisible to me. I remember saying, 'Goodnight all,' and hearing the answering grunts of the other three. The next thing I knew was Leningrad.

EIGHT

I woke to see that bluish-white light on the ceiling that indicates a covering of snow outside. But the ceiling puzzled me. It was like no other ceiling I'd woken under. Then I began to make sense of it all. I was on a train. Dickon was in the bunk above me. We were approaching Leningrad. The wheels were making the same sound as I slowly came to my senses as they had been making when I fell asleep. Truck-truck, truck-truck. Truck-truck, truck-truck. At the same unhurrying, but unstoppable, speed.

The four of us got dressed in a tight entangled way, as I imagined Houdini might have done prior to escaping from a box. We took turns at the wash-basin. Dick and I exchanged cryptic smiles at that point, smiles we hoped were invisible to the others but, in that confined space, probably were not. The big window inside our compartment was, for obvious reasons, of frosted glass, so it was not until we were out in the corridor and queuing for the toilet that we got our first sight of Leningrad. We were still some fifteen minutes away from our destination, the city's Moscow station. We saw grey factories and grey apartment blocks, and railway yards in which infinite lines of goods wagons waited patiently for something, with snow upon their roofs. Near at hand fresh snow carpeted the railway tracks. It hid the sleepers completely; all that stood out were the long dark parallels of the rails themselves, occasionally weaving through each other via sets of points. But this was Leningrad. Peter the Great's wide window on the west: Russia's pre-revolutionary capital, St Petersburg.

The city came into its own once we'd arrived at the huge station and got the other side of it. The long broad perspective of Nevsky Prospekt stretched before us, a model of refined elegance that equalled anything in Edinburgh or Paris. Our hotel, the finest we'd encountered yet, lay just off that immense main street.

Natasha did something wonderful. She came up to Dick and me just as we all entered the hotel lobby and said, 'You will have a twin-bed room together. I talked to the hotel staff. It is on the second floor. Number two-three-four. All the others are on the first.' She had said all this in that unsmiling way we were getting used to seeing everywhere around us. But when she finished making her bald but beautiful announcement I saw her mouth twitch and move up at the corners. Her eyes gave a mischievous twinkle, but then she turned away abruptly, as if her face might get out of hand if she allowed it to start smiling, and went to talk in a businesslike way to someone else.

Our room was lovely, by far the grandest and most comfortable we'd stayed in yet. We each threw ourselves down onto separate beds and bounced around a bit, revelling in the spaciousness, after the confined compartment on the sleeper train, revelling in the privacy, revelling in our togetherness. Then I jumped up and threw myself down on top of Dickon and, still dressed for outdoors, we bounced around a bit and kissed deeply and squeezed each other's erections through our overcoats.

'Shower before breakfast,' said Dickon, taking charge suddenly. 'Let's go for it.' We got up off the bed and took our clothes off and then we 'went for it'. Not just for the shower, but for all the intimacy that we'd got used to in our shower in Suzdal and had missed for forty hours. We came so explosively that our spurtings were this time not hosed downward by the running shower water, but hit the inside walls of the shower at waist height and had to be wiped off with flannels when we'd finished. Then, trying to look as though butter wouldn't melt in our mouths and with hair still wet, we went down and joined the other fourteen for breakfast.

And then, once again, we packed into a bus. We weren't complaining. We were being driven around one of the most magnificent cities of Europe.

Peter the Great had built his new capital on a raft of boggy islets at the edge of the sea. At the narrow end of an inlet from the Gulf of Finland, itself an inlet of the Baltic Sea, in the delta of the River Neva. His model was Venice of course. And although I'd never been to Venice I knew it from pictures and the similarities were obvious. As we drove the length of Nevsky Prospekt, heading towards the open sea, we crossed canal after canal: each waterfront was lined with row upon row of handsome Renaissance mansions and palaces. They looked even better for the snow that had come overnight. It gave form to their roofscapes and lay thick along the frozen surfaces of the canals outside their front doors. When we reached the sea at last, well, there was snow even on the sea.

Snow lay on the beaches, and on the ice that went out a little way. A few yards off the shore the ice was broken into snow-topped floes that moved a little, though only a little, as the currents of the Neva estuary jostled with those of the open sea.

'How does this compare with Venice?' I asked Dickon. I knew that he had been there.

'Venice is smaller. Prettier.' He'd answered without hesitation. He must have prepared his thoughts as we drove along. 'This is majestic. Huge.' He squeezed my knee. It was safe to assume that no-one was looking at us; all were focused, spellbound, on the panorama unfolding outside.

We stopped on the big open space beside the water that was Palace Embankment. Next to us the waters of the Neva were growing salty as they met the sea and on the far side, perhaps half a mile away we could see the gilded spire of the St Peter and Paul cathedral rising above the trees and the massive fortress walls. The cathedral spire, cleaving the sky above, seemed sharp and pointed as a hypodermic syringe.

Near at hand was moored the cruiser Aurora, serendipitously named for the dawn. She had famously fired the first shots at the façade of the Winter Palace in October 1917, symbolically ushering in the Communists' new day.

A stone's-throw away was the Winter Palace itself. Its

façade was painted partly white but mainly green. A green of an unsettling kind that I had seen a lot in Russia but nowhere else I'd been. The colour was nostalgic, somehow. It was the colour of foliage at the end of summer perhaps, but also redolent of verdigris and bile. It didn't seem a suitable colour for a building, I thought. Yet both the Imperial Russians of old and the Communists of today clearly thought it an ideal colour. So who was I to disagree?

When you looked closely at the paintwork you could see that it was cracked and, in places, flaking away. All that salt in the air, of course. Venice yet again. Its rococo-framed windows had a blank, sad, widowed look about them. That was purely subjective, though. The palace was now part of the Hermitage museum, but I knew what it had once been and a sudden sadness descended on me. In that haunted place, the Palace Embankment, I felt overwhelmed with all the ghosts of anguished history.

I had every reason to feel happy, walking around that famous, beautiful waterside with Dickon next to me. It was a moment of my life that would be with me always, I well knew. And yet... Dickon and I had embarked on something. We'd slept together, we were having sex together as often as we could. We were wonderful friends... Friends was as far as my mind dared go. We hadn't begun to talk about any of this. We would be spending six more nights and days together. But then...? Already parting loomed ahead of us, when we'd only just properly met. On the only occasion the subject of sexuality had come up in conversation between us we had both proclaimed ourselves straight. This might need revisiting at some point, I thought, in the light of what had happened since. But opening up that subject would be very fraught. I wasn't ready for such a potentially dangerous conversation and so I was carefully keeping my mouth shut. To judge from his own silence on the subject Dickon was in the same boat, probably having the same thoughts.

Natasha turned to face the group. She explained why the Hermitage was called the Hermitage. 'A hermitage,' she announced, 'is a place where a nuck lives.'

'A nuck?' queried Jenny. 'Do you mean a monk?'

'No,' Natasha insisted. 'A nuck is a small animal. It is not a monk.'

Dickon thought he'd got it. 'You mean a hermit crab. It lives in the sea and lives in other animals' shells.'

Natasha was unimpressed. 'It is not a crab. It does not live in the sea.'

'A kind of beetle,' kindly suggested Professor Sykes, the don from York whose Russian was rather good.

Natasha leapt at that. 'Yes,' she said, almost smiling her relief. 'It is a peakle.'

'A pickle?' offered Dickon mischievously. I nudged him in the ribs and said shut up.

'A   beetle,'   corrected   Sykes gently.

Natasha accepted the correction with grace. 'Ah. A peetle. Yes.' And a peetle it remained for ever afterwards.

In the afternoon Dick and I changed some travellers' cheques into roubles in a Berioska shop. Then we returned to our hotel and went to bed.

'It must be eight inches long,' I said.

'And yours must be a good seven and a half.'

'I don't know,' I said doubtfully. 'The last time I measured it was back at school and then it was six.'

'Don't remember when I last measured mine,' Dickon mumbled, sounding a bit awkward about it. I strongly suspected that he wasn't telling the truth but I certainly wasn't going to care if that was the case. We were lying naked together on my bed (the luxury of a centrally heated bedroom when there is snow outside!) and for the umpteenth time minutely exploring the contours of each other's bollocks and ramrod pricks. Granted, mine was a half inch shorter than Dick's was, but I was mightily impressed by the look of them both. They both seemed longer this afternoon than they had been previously. Was it conceivable that they'd grown in the last week?

When it came to our balls, though, where size was concerned mine had the edge … if items of that particular shape could be said to have an edge. My limited experience was that unlike cocks, which were of infinite variety where size and shape were concerned, bollocks tended to come in two main sizes: the small kind and the large kind. Mine were of the large kind and Dickon's the small kind. The knowledge that he couldn't be bigger and better than me in absolutely everything was gratifying and somehow also touching.

As if to reinforce my appreciation of this happy detail I spent some time caressing those smaller-than-mine treasures of Dickon's with my fingers before starting to masturbate his cock. But when I did start slowly to run my clasped hand up and down its length he stopped my hand with his. With his free one. The other one was lightly exploring my buttock cleft.

'Wait,' Dickon said. And I heard that appealing note of diffidence come into his voice. The one that was there when he was about to say something he wasn't sure I'd go along with. 'Do you want to go the whole way this time?'

Involuntarily I drew in my breath. 'You mean fuck.'

Dickon said diffidently, 'Only if you'd like.'

'I've never been fucked,' I said. My tone was neutral, flat.

'Me neither,' said Dickon. His tone was also flat and neutral. Neither of us wanted to give all of it away at once.

But it was going to have to come out. Now. 'I've never fucked anyone,' I said.

'Nor have I,' said Dickon in a wisp of a voice.

'Girls?' I asked neutrally. Though only my voice was in neutral. My feelings were revving all over the place.

'No,' said Dickon. He made it sound like an achievement. Like having given up cigarettes.

I said, 'These days we're supposed to wear…'

'I know,' said Dickon. 'But if neither of us has ever…'

'I agree,' I said. 'The rule doesn't apply to us.'

'Anyway,' said Dickon, 'there weren't any in the Berioska shop.'

We giggled inordinately at that, releasing some of the tension that had been building up.

'So do you want to…?' Dickon tailed awkwardly off.

'You mean which way,' I helped him out. 'Both I think.'

'For me too,' Dickon said.

The final detail remained to be decided. I saved a bit of time by cutting to the chase. 'Since you've already got your finger halfway into my anus you might as well go first.'

'Then lie on your tummy,' Dickon said. He climbed out from under me (up to then I'd been lying on my tummy on *his* tummy – now I lay on my tummy on the bed) and he climbed aboard my back.

There was a short spell of trial and error, during which I began to fear I'd lose my own load involuntarily all over the nice hotel bedspread. We learned together, though. Me to spread my legs a little and helpfully raise my arse. Dickon to relax me with a finger and to apply liberal quantities of spit.

It hurt a bit, I had to admit that. Dick's dick was not just long but also thick. Yet what a place to find yourself when the moment came to lose your cherry! In an elegant hotel bedroom, warm and comfortable, but with a view outside of the snow-covered grand buildings of Leningrad, the magical old capital city of the Russia of Peter the Great.

It all came to a climax quite suddenly. I felt Dick's cock swell inside me then burst. And then, though I wasn't even touching it – it must have been the pressure of Dickon's thrusting that was rubbing it against the bedspread – my own cock emptied itself suddenly – there was nothing I could do about it – and poured my semen out all over the top of the bed.

Up to that moment it had seemed certain that as soon as we'd both ejaculated we'd want to reverse roles and repeat the procedure, this time with me on top and my cock plumbing Dickon's arse. But now the moment had come, and we'd both come, we found we didn't want to do that at all. We just wanted to get into bed together and hold each other and cuddle each other to sleep. And so we did just that. Though we did our best to clean up the bedspread first. And had a shower. And I prudently sat on the toilet for a bit.

When we woke up it was nearly time for dinner. Before we got out of bed and while we still had our arms around each other I looked Dickon directly in the face. I needed to say something. 'It's not just physical, is it.' I said.

'No it's not,' Dickon said. We both sounded very certain of that.

'It's not just sex,' I added for good measure.

'No,' said Dickon. 'It's more than that.'

And that was as far as the conversation went. That was as far as it could go at that time. We weren't ready to let it go further than that. Further than that would have been frightening. We couldn't have handled it. We gave each other a collusive squeeze and a businesslike kiss. Then we got out of bed and got dressed.

NINE

We went for a walk after dinner. All sixteen of us. We were escorted by two friends of Natasha's, one female one male. They were both good-looking and outgoing. Very not-Moscow. Very Leningrad. We'd learned today that Natasha's home town was Leningrad; Moscow was where her work took her fortnightly. She too was changing, I though, in her westward-looking home town.

Sunset was happening as we set out. We were walking along Nevsky Prospekt as the golden ball went blazing down. Streetlamps came on and the city's aspect changed. It had been magical by daylight. By night it became a fairytale. But what a fairytale! Thousands of workers had perished simply in the building of it. It had been the cradle of no less than three bloody revolutions, and just twenty-five years before I was born its people had been driven to starvation and cannibalism during Hitler's mad siege.

Nevsky Prospekt, Nevsky Prospekt. Was ever there a walk so long?! Yet we gloried in every minute of it as Natasha's informative, cheerful friends pointed out places of fascination along the way. We turned off the main thoroughfare and walked the pathway beside the frozen Moika Canal. We came to the Yusupov Palace and heard the story – which everyone knew – of what had happened there.

Everyone knows the story of Rasputin. How his

influence on the royal family, and particularly on Tsarina Alexandra, was threatening to destabilise not just the monarchy but also the entire state. How the death of Rasputin became a political necessity. How the gentle Prince Felix Yusupov reluctantly led a conspiracy to carry it out. How Rasputin was tricked into going to the Yusupov Palace late one December evening in 1916 ... the bait being a pretty young girl. Rasputin was not good at resisting the allure of pretty females...

He was taken down to the basement of the palace outside which we now stood on the frozen towpath, and offered cakes and wine while he waited for the girl. He didn't eat or drink at first but then he did. Full of potassium cyanide, those baits should have done the trick, but they did not. Felix and his co-conspirators shot Rasputin inside the palace but still he did not die. He crawled into the courtyard and was shot again, and kicked in the head, and bludgeoned till he was comatose.

For this moment – which came several harrowing hours later than scheduled – there was already a plan. Rasputin's body was to be disposed of beneath the ice of one of the canals. It couldn't be done immediately outside the palace: the ice on the Moika Canal was too thick. (We looked down at it. The ice had been thick and snow-covered that night in December 1916; it was thick and snow-covered now.) Besides, the police station stood right opposite. An officer on duty had already come round to the palace to ask about the shots. A car backfiring, they told him and he went away. Cars backfired a lot in 1916. They took Rasputin's body to a place they'd already reconnoitred, where the ice was thin. We walked there now…

All the way to the River Neva. Across the bridge to the island opposite. From there another bridge led across the Malaya Neva, the Lesser Neva: the Petrovsky Bridge. We stood upon that bridge. We looked down at the ice-floes gliding past slowly, nudging each other and groaning as they went with the current. From this spot the body of Rasputin had been tipped through a hole in the December ice.

His body, when the police fished it out the next morning, showed signs that he'd still been alive when he was thrown in. I stood on this spot above the Neva and felt the marrow in my bones grow cold. My temples throbbed with cold and my teeth started to chatter. I felt Dick's arm come round me. 'Are you OK?' he said.

'Yes,' I said. The only possible answer for anyone English. 'It's just… Well, it's very cold.'

'Yes,' said Dick, with a warmth in his voice that immediately made me feel a bit less chilled. 'And a bit spooky too, don't you think? But I'll get you warm when we're back at the hotel.'

But that wasn't to be just yet. According to the Russian Orthodox Church calendar today was Holy Saturday. Tonight was the Vigil of Easter. Midnight, an hour or so from now, would see the beginning of the feast of Christ's Resurrection, Easter Day. Some of the churches in Leningrad were operational – Natasha referred to them as working churches – and would be holding processions with all the eastern pomp and ceremony that those entailed. Our guides asked if we wanted to witness one. We said yes, of course.

Around a labyrinth of streets we found our way at last to a church. The crowds pressed thick around. A procession, with mitred bishop, a canopy, swinging censers, robed deacons and all the rest, was trying to make its way towards the church, like a caterpillar through a swarm of ants. Some of the big crowd was friendly – religious or simply supportive; some of it was hostile. It was hard to make out in the darkness who was on which side. There were shouts and arguments that regularly drowned out the chanting, which was far from feeble, of the religious members of the crowd. Fireworks were thrown dangerously into the crowd, exploding among the trapped procession with bursts of noise and flame.

We were hemmed in, and being jostled, on all sides. A light went on high up in a building across the road. It was quickly switched off again. But I just had time to register the silhouette of a man looking out of that window, binoculars to his eyes, watching the crowd, watching the procession... And watching us.

'It could be dangerous,' said one of our guides. 'We're taking you back to your hotel.' We didn't protest or argue. This wasn't our dispute (or so we thought at the time) and our watches by now were showing twelve thirty. It was certainly time to go.

But the city, which had seemed quiet enough earlier, seemed suddenly to have come alive. The trolley-buses were jam-packed and so were the trams. We threaded our way through hordes of pedestrians, went tripping over tram rails... We were no longer sixteen. Our group had got split up, then split again. At last there were just Dickon and me, ducking and diving together through a moving crowd.

We had no idea where we were. We walked, at times we ran. At last, somehow, we tumbled out of a back street into Nevsky Prospekt. I'd never in my life imagined that the sight of the street name, Nevsky Prospekt, high on a wall in Cyrillic script, would fill me with the emotion that is reserved for the experience of Coming Home. It was at that moment that I felt Dickon's gloved hand clasp mine. We turned the right way – we knew that for certain – and then had the never-to-be-forgotten experience of walking together down the crowded main thoroughfare of Russia's greatest city, at one in the morning on Easter Day, publicly hand in hand.

We weren't the first to make it back to the hotel, but we weren't the last. We all got back together again eventually, waiting up in the hotel bar till two a.m. We drank vodka there, shared our stories of getting lost in Leningrad, and laughed at ourselves until, at three in the morning, bed could no longer be postponed.

'I think I caught a chill last night,' I told Dickon the next morning, a few minutes after I'd disentangled myself from his arms.

'I'm not surprised,' he said. 'Standing on the Petrovsky bridge in all that snow... Your teeth were chattering.'

'It was as though the cold was coming up from the river below,' I said, 'and getting right into my bones.' I did know that warm air rises and cold air sinks, yet that was how it had felt at the time.

'I've got some Aspirin,' Dickon said. 'Take three and you'll be fine.' He rummaged in his sponge-bag and handed the packet to me. I swallowed them gratefully.

We spent the morning in St Isaac's Cathedral – one of the least charming buildings in Leningrad – but the afternoon was better. We went to the Hermitage. Named, as we kept remembering, after the famous peetle's home. The Winter Palace forms a part only of this largest art gallery in the world. It had been knocked through into adjacent buildings that were almost equally as grand. The sheer number of works of art was a daunting thing. Great masters – a few Constables had found their way there among the others, to my surprise – lined every wall. And there was a room for every day of the year.

My brain gave up after a while. My thoughts turned to the building itself: the Winter Palace. The palace from which the Provisional Government, led by Kerensky, had emerged, hands in air, in response to the shelling of its front wall by the Aurora in the river outside. The palace in which Nicholas II and Alexandra had held their coronation ball. The palace into which the mangled body of Alexander III had been brought after his carriage had been bombed in the city streets, and where he'd shortly died…

I looked from a window into a small weed-grown courtyard far below. Once it had been the Imperial family's rose garden. No roses grew there now. Among rubble and the tracks of tractor tyres in the snow a rather grand, old-fashioned bath-tub lay abandoned down there. Was that the bath in which Alexandra had bathed? Or Nicholas? The one in which their daughters, Olga, Tatiana, Maria and Anastasia had been allowed to take only cold baths … because their mother knew they mustn't take their privileged life for granted, they needed to share what ordinary people underwent day to day and were not to be spoiled. I had a return of the feeling I'd had on the Petrovsky bridge. A feeling of cold rushing upwards at me. A cold that came blowing up from the past, from the chill halls of history, from the grave.

'Are you all right?' It was Dickon of course, coming to find me, looking out for me.

'Not really,' I said. 'I just keep suddenly feeling cold.'

'We'll give you some more Aspirin when we get back. You'll be right as rain.'

'You're great,' I said, and touched his cheek with the back of my hand.

I did take those Aspirin when we got back. After dinner I felt slightly better but nevertheless, didn't feel like going out to a bar afterwards with most of the others. Dickon stayed in with me – I was rather disproportionately touched by that – and we climbed into the warmest place we knew. By now it was our favourite place. Dickon's bed. Which was also mine.

By the morning I was feeling stronger, and ready for the drive we made in the bus, out into the countryside. Our destination was the country cottage in which Lenin had stayed, following his return from exile during the revolutionary period. The cottage was deep in birch woods, and we trekked along a path among the trees from the spot where our bus had parked. As soon as we saw the cottage we all roared with laughter. The entire building was preserved in a glass case.

We went to a party in the evening. We were the guests of the Leningrad Konsomols, the Young Communists. Our hosts were lads and girls of about our own age. Like the Young Farmers or the Senior Scouts. There was beer and sandwiches in a barn-like building that resembled a village hall. Our hosts were very welcoming and gracious, but none of them spoke more than a few words of English, and most of them not even that. In our proficiency in each other's language our two groups were very evenly matched. We had to entertain each other without words.

There was a grand piano in the middle of the hall.

During the awkward lull after the sandwiches were gone and nobody was speaking to anybody else Dickon strode off towards the instrument without saying anything to me and, to my great surprise, sat down at it and opened the keyboard lid. He launched into a tune from Rigoletto in a very simple arrangement. Then he played a second one. He was not an advanced pianist. But I had no idea he could even do that. The subject had never come up between us. I was very impressed.

After a third extract from the Verdi opera Dickon had to give up. His repertoire had clearly run its course. The question, 'Can anyone else…?' ricocheted around. I found myself walking towards the instrument; it was hardly a conscious decision. On my way towards the piano stool I passed Dickon on his way back. Like a batsman going in to the wicket, passing his team-mate who has been got out.

'Well done,' I said to Dickon out of the corner of my mouth.

'Good luck, mate,' he said out of the corner of his. We didn't stop to chat.

I wasn't a brilliant pianist either. I had once been able to play the whole of Für Elise from memory. I knew I would be able to remember the beginning of it. What would happen when I got into the deeper waters in the middle of it, though, was anybody's guess. I sat down, took a deep breath and launched into it.

The acoustic of the barn-like space was enormous. My

opening phrase came out at an orchestral level of decibels. I had no choice except to keep going, I thought, like a tractor through mud, until the limitations of my memory forced me to come to a stop. But to my great surprise that didn't happen. Every note seemed to have been stored in my muscle memory, and I didn't falter or hesitate but went on going all the way to the end that Beethoven had assigned to the piece. To my even greater surprise, when I'd finished, everybody clapped. They must have applauded Dickon too, I realised. I mean, we all must have. Strangely I found I had no memory of that.

I left the piano stool and walked back to the others, grinning idiotically, I think. No, I said repeatedly to people who kindly asked me, there was nothing else I could play without the music. By now someone else was at the piano. Jenny's friend Teresa turned out to have a string of Schubert polkas stored in her memory and she trotted them all out. She was really rather splendid. None of the rest of us had any idea she could do that.

When Teresa had run out of Schubert a heavily built Russian chap ascended the stool and played some very dark and gloomy tunes while the rest of us re-arranged the furniture and played a game of musical chairs. There was something wonderfully crazy, surreally absurd, about playing musical chairs with a squad of nineteen-year-old Party members.

It certainly broke the social ice. After that we taught our new friends the Hokey Cokey, which became quite energetic, and they taught us an intricate Russian dance.

We ended with Strip the Willow. Our goodbyes were warm and smiley, but it was a bit of a relief to return to our hotel. The evening had been a bit of an effort. The lack of a common language had prevented it from being a total success.

On the other hand, there had been one good result as far as I was concerned. If I was still nursing a chill or harbouring a cold, I'd managed to forget the fact.

Back in bed with Dickon I felt I'd come home; I'd found the place where I was meant to be. But I couldn't stop myself from counting the days ahead. After this one we were only going to be sharing a bed for three more nights.

TEN

I still hadn't fucked Dickon. I didn't do it that night. I wondered whether I'd cross that Rubicon before our time in Russia came to an end. Or after that...

We still hadn't mentioned after that. We hadn't mentioned any possible future for us. Afraid of the subject. Afraid there might not be an after that. Afraid there might not be an us.

In four days' time we would be back in England. Back at our parents' houses. Those were both in the south of England. But the south of England was a big place. Though the country is only about seventy miles across at its northern neck, it's about three hundred miles across its southern sweep. Dickon's parents lived in the south west, near Exeter, while mine lived near Canterbury in the south east. We'd exchanged that information while we were still at Heathrow, minutes after we'd first met. Back then it had been a matter of mere polite interest; we hadn't dreamed that within ten days it would be an important logistical issue with consequences for the future of our – I have to put it in inverted commas – "relationship".

A week after returning to those poles apart places we would both be going back up north for the start of the summer term. Me at Durham, Dick at Edinburgh. Actually, although the two cities were over a hundred miles apart the same train line out of London served both of them. I wondered whether we might arrange to travel up on the same train… I then thought how tantalising and frustrating this would be. Yes, these were the nineteen-eighties, not the eighteen-eighties, but you still didn't see pairs of lads kissing and fondling each other in the carriages of the east coast main line. We still weren't discussing any of this. These were just my private thoughts, kept to myself. But I knew somehow, I was absolutely certain, that they were shared in every detail by Dickon. We just weren't able to open that part of ourselves up to each other.

But for now… For now we had now. And since none of us know what the future holds, not even certain if we will be alive in one day's time let alone happy, that is the best that we could ever say.

We went to the Peter and Paul Fortress. The sun shone and I felt quite bright. The fortress was on an island of its own, with a star-shaped ground plan and walls so thick and powerful that from the outside that was all we could see, except for the golden hypodermic spire of the cathedral rising above. But once inside we found ourselves once again in a town within a town. Like the Moscow Kremlin the complex contained streets full of historic buildings. But unlike the Kremlin with its medieval churches and onion domes the buildings within the fortress were recognisably Renaissance and western. Peter the Great had built the fortress at the beginning of the eighteenth century – it was the earliest part of his new capital – and thanks to its impregnability it had changed very little since. On its high walls we stood and looked back across the floe-ridden river at the Winter Palace on its embankment and the rooftops, spires and domes of the city beyond.

I made it bravely through the morning but needed a rest in the afternoon. Dick decided I needed to do this in peace and (there was some reluctance on both our parts) let me be and went out for a walk with Jenny and the others. Alone in the hotel room I found myself thinking about Dick's friendship with Jenny, and about my friendship with Jenny, wondering how much my new ... thing ... with Dick would change things there...

...And woke up to find Dick back in the room, telling me it was time to get up and shower as it was nearly time for dinner. I'd slept for over three hours. But that had done the trick. I felt much better. Dickon and I showered together and helped each other ejaculate happily under the running water.

One more new city remained on our itinerary. Veliky Novgorod, or Novgorod the Great. It lay a hundred and twenty miles south of Leningrad, back on the road to Moscow. In order to get there, see the place and get back to Leningrad all in one day, we climbed into our bus at seven o'clock the next morning. I hardly knew how I was going to survive the day, but Novgorod was a city I had determined to see, and might not get another chance again in my lifetime. And I had Dickon with me, to prop me up if need be, and to ply me with Aspirin.

Novgorod the Great was massively historical. An early Viking settlement, it had become one of the major trading towns of the Hanseatic League, the capital of one of the principalities that later merged to become Russia, and – for a period – it had been the capital of a republic. A republic was a rare thing five hundred years ago.

It was hot in the bus, and our picnic breakfast seemed dry as ashes. I'd somehow developed a hacking cough. But Novgorod was worth the trip. The town was eye-wateringly beautiful. The sun was out, the wind was light, the snow was thawing rapidly, the melt-water sparkled in the sun as it flowed and dropped. I felt the sun's heat through my overcoat; winter had turned to spring overnight. I might have felt like dying when we climbed aboard the bus at seven o'clock in the early light but arrival in Novgorod and the wonderful sight of it – like Suzdal it was a small and fairytale city set in the middle of the countryside – cured me of any ailments I might have had.

Dickon and I competed to turn cartwheels on the grass sward outside the old monastery that stood where the river merged with the lake, and we tramped happily around the timber churches in the wood. In the benevolent warmth of the sun my hacking cough had disappeared as quickly as it had come.

We spent the afternoon in the Kremlin. In my ignorance I'd thought the Kremlin was a place that was unique to Moscow. It was not. The word Kremlin was simply an approximate equivalent to citadel. Every historic Russian town had one. In the heart of

Novgorod's Kremlin there was a music school. Because of the sudden spring warmth all the windows had been flung joyously open and music flowed out of them in unstoppable streams. Strings, brass, woodwind, pianos and percussion, all practising different works, classical, modern and romantic, in different tempi and clashing keys. The exuberant energy of his happy hullaballoo was glorious.

The cathedral in the Kremlin was, Natasha told us, the oldest in Russia. Lovely inside and, like the other medieval churches we'd been into, cosy. We climbed up into a library that was housed in a high room above the church and saw a collection of ancient Russian books, illuminated parchment manuscripts. They were shown off to us with pride. They were in great condition, looked after according to the most up-to-date principles of conservation. 'I didn't think they'd kept any of this,' Dickon said to me.

'Neither did I,' I had to answer. Modern, Communist, Russia's relationship with its historic past was turning out to be more complex than I'd thought.

Then we walked around a part of the surrounding rampart wall. Dickon and I kept looking at each other during this walk. We were both remembering our epoch-making walk around the walls of Suzdal in the dark, pursued by dogs... How that had been the start of everything... The start of everything. Whatever everything was.

Novgorod had a magnificent lake. It had a lakeside

beach. We went down there in the early evening sun. The local lads were playing on the ice-floes. They would pick up a plank of wood, use it as a gang-plank to board a nearby floe and then pull up their drawbridge and use it as a pole to punt the floe out into the lake. Dickon and I tried it, and so did some of the other lads in our party. We weren't brave enough to go very far out. But the more expert local boys went skimming along the edge of the river and out into the lake, going quite a distance and getting up a good rate of knots.

We were back on the beach and trying to stamp the warmth back into our ice-chilled feet when Dickon said suddenly, 'Give me your arm.' We linked our arms together and did an impromptu dance in front of the others. It might have looked a bit Russian but it probably didn't. It might have a looked a bit gay … and it evidently did. We attracted quite a few shouts and whistles from the boys on the ice floes, and after a minute we stopped. Our own party simply laughed. It was OK to be gay at British universities in 1986. But I wasn't sure if the same went for small-town Russia.

Nothing is as quickly forgotten as pain and illness. At the end of that happy day in the sunshine at Novgorod I could barely remember how ill I'd felt that morning when we'd set out at seven o'clock. But as the day's warmth waned and night came slowly down during the three-and-a-half-hour bus journey back to Leningrad the memory came back. So did the cough.

But a good night's sleep with Dickon in bed with me put things right again. I woke up feeling rested, and showered with Dick before breakfast. We didn't bring each other off in the shower this time. We'd just done that before getting out of bed.

This was to be our last day in Leningrad. Our last full day in the USSR. This evening we would board the sleeper back to Moscow and tomorrow morning return to London. There Dickon and I would part...

We still hadn't broached the two big frightening topics. What was going to happen to us after that? What had already happened to us? We both knew how monumental those questions were. I could see that Dickon shared my thoughts; every time he looked at me they were written on his face. But neither of us had the remotest idea what we could say about them. Perhaps it would all become clear when we said our goodbyes at Heathrow airport. Perhaps at that moment some inspired words would come to one or both of us and for better or worse we'd blurt it all out. Dear God, I thought, that moment lay little more than twenty-four hours off!

Our final day was to be a day of gilded palaces. We headed out of town a few miles towards the suburb of Pushkin. Those who know the story of the Russian royal family will know the area better as Tsarskoye Selo. In the huge park there were still two palaces. One was the early eighteenth-century Catherine Palace, which had been beautifully and expensively restored following bomb damage in the Second World War. The other was the slightly junior Alexander Palace, the refuge of Nicholas II and Alexandra during the final turbulent years of the Tsarist regime. You could see why they liked the place. Even today the grounds were an oasis of calm countryside with views across to the quietly flowing Neva. We mounted the grand flight of steps up to the front door of the Catherine Palace.

Everywhere was clean white, blue and gold. State rooms were high and full of Corinthian pillars – with gilded capitals of course. As I walked around the rooms I felt a sense of elation. I seemed to be walking about six inches above the floor.

Dick had given me my now customary Aspirin at lunchtime, before we set out. He'd given me a nip of Vodka just after that. In the bus I'd complained of a bad headache and kind Professor Sykes had given me two tablets called Veganin... I'd never heard of those, but accepted them gratefully and took them with a swig of water from a bottle that one of us had. So I floated round the gorgeous Catherine Palace and then floated back to the bus. My headache began to worsen as we drove off. Natasha, concerned for me, gave me two Russian painkillers to take. I didn't mention the Aspirin, the Veganin and the Vodka. Just in case she withdrew the offer. I accepted them gratefully and wolfed them down.

We were only driving a couple of miles this time. Our destination was the palace at Pavlovsk. Another beautiful creation commanded by Catherine the Great. I approved its elegant design from the outside only. I felt too unwell to get out of the bus. While the others went round the palace I lay on the bus's back seat. I closed my eyes and found my head a whirl of wraith-like Mongol or Tartar warriors with golden helmets. Then mercifully

I was asleep.

That sleep did me some good. I was woken by the bustle of the others coming back on board the bus. I found I was able to sit up for the journey back. Well, I sat up only up to a point. I sat next to Dickon of course. I leaned against him, snuggled into him, and he snuggled against me too. He put an arm around me protectively and the others smiled indulgently at that, without comment. I managed not to cough too much as I laid my head against Dick's shoulder and into his cheek. Instead I had a nosebleed all down his shirt.

Yet dinner, our last dinner at our nice hotel in Leningrad, perked me up remarkably. I felt well able to join the others for the final entertainment of the trip: a visit to the ballet at the Mikhailovsky theatre in Art Square, just off Nevsky Prospekt.

The theatre was another gilded palace – the oldest theatre in the city. We had two boxes between the sixteen of us, and watched and heard Swan Lake. I thought the whole evening was magnificent. It was hard to believe that in twelve hours' time I would be on a plane bound for England. Eight hours after that I would be back in the comfort of my parents' house. If I was still unwell I could visit the doctor the morning after that. Those were partly comforting, partly confusing, thoughts. Another loomed among them, though, that was dreadful. I would no longer have Dickon with me. As the wild swans finally flew off on stage below me I gave Dick's leg a meaningful caress and he returned it.

I didn't feel like partying when we got on board the sleeper. Dickon undressed me and put me into my bunk even before the train pulled out. Then, not without some feelings of guilt – he said – he joined the others in the corridor for farewell celebratory wine and vodka, and tea from the charcoal stove that had indissoluble cubes of sugar in it.

Every few minutes Dick popped back into the compartment to see how I was. 'Do you want the door shut?' he asked each time. 'It's a bit noisy out there.'

'Leave the door open,' I said each time. I was conscious that my voice was becoming more and more of a croak. And speaking made me cough. Actually, not speaking also made me cough. Everything made me cough.

'It's very claustrophobic if I'm shut in,' I said. 'And it's also incredibly hot. You must have noticed.'

'Hmm,' said Dick. 'It's certainly warm enough. But hot...?' He laid his cool hand on my forehead. After a few seconds he ran it down my cheek. Then it travelled, as if it had its own agenda, beneath the blankets, down my chest and tummy. Dick's fingers tickled my pubes for a bit, then they found my cock.

I realised as he handled it that it had grown very small and shrunk. 'Hot?' he said. 'It's you that's hot. In more ways than one.'

'My cock's not hot,' I said.

'It is in terms of temperature,' Dick said. 'And whatever state it's in apart from that it's still nice. Don't worry. Get to sleep now. Tomorrow we'll get you sorted out.'

I did get off to sleep eventually. The happy chatter in the corridor faded gradually, along with the wheels' truck-truck, truck-truck. I didn't hear Dick and the others come in and go to bed in their bunks. And in the morning I did get sorted out. Though not in quite the way that either Dick or I might have hoped.

ELEVEN

Dickon hauled me out of my bunk in the morning. I leaned against the compartment's frosted-glass window while he pulled on my underpants and socks. The other two lads politely left the compartment to the two of us after asking, equally politely, if Dickon needed any help. He told them he could manage me on his own.

He got my jeans on, and my shirt. Did up my shoes. Wriggled my pullover down over my head and shoulders. He stowed my sponge-bag in my suitcase. Then he put on my overcoat and buttoned it up. Then he kissed my lips. 'Don't cry,' he said. 'You'll be all right.'

I hadn't known I was crying. That took me by surprise a bit.

The doors opened as soon as the train had come to a stop. At that point Dickon did need help. He gave my suitcase to one of the Durham lads to carry along the platform. Then he enlisted Jenny's support – quite literally. I walked between them as, one on each side of me, they propped me up.

'Natasha mustn't see him like this,' Dickon said. He was now fully in charge of me. 'Walk in front of him,' he commanded another of our travelling companions. 'Don't let Natasha see his face, or that he can't walk.'

How long the platform of Moscow's Leningrad station was! Dickon had said that I couldn't walk. Yet somehow I did. I forced my legs to move, putting one foot in front of the other, while on either side of me Dick and Jenny somehow took all of my weight, like flying buttresses; their shoulders pressed hard against mine, while their arms met each other's around my waist.

We walked out of the concourse towards the waiting bus. The doors to its luggage hold stood open expectantly. 'Get his suitcase into the hold quickly,' Dick told the guy who was carrying it. 'See it gets on first. Make sure the other cases go on top of it.' My Durham pal hurried towards the bus to carry those instructions out. He put his own suitcase on top of mine, then came back to relieve Jenny and Dickon of their own luggage so that they, still moving slowly towards the bus with me between them, could get me on board and into a seat. Before Natasha could see what sort of a state I was in.

It nearly worked. We were at the foot of the bus's steps. Dickon had bent down and was lifting my right foot onto the bottommost step. Then there Natasha was. She only needed a half second's look to see what the situation was. 'Oh Oliver. You are all red. You can not travel to England like that. We must get a doctor at once.'

'Natasha, no,' said Dickon. 'Just let him get the flight.'

'I'll be fine once I'm on the aeroplane,' I said. I managed to speak strongly and to sound quite upbeat. 'I'll see a doctor as soon as I get to England.'

'No,' Natasha said very firmly. 'You must see a doctor first.'

Natasha spoke to the driver of the bus. She spoke to an official who had just walked up. A moment later we were all walking away from the bus. The official, and Natasha, led us into a private waiting room between the concourse and the bus park. Probably it was normally used for visiting VIPs, I guessed, and for Party top brass.

We sat in armchairs – some of us. Others stood. In an incredibly short space of time the doctor turned up. In front of all the others she examined me. The standard initial examination that I was familiar with. She looked into my eyes, felt my hands and peered at my finger nails. She took my temperature and felt my pulse. Then she turned to Natasha and spoke.

Immediately Natasha told me what she said. 'Oh Oliver, the doctor says it is very terrible. You must go at once to the hospital.'

'No, Natasha,' I protested. 'I must get on the plane. I will see a doctor in England.'

The doctor spoke again to Natasha in Russian. Again Natasha translated. 'The doctor says if you go on the plane you will not get to England.'

It was at the sound of those last words that my will finally failed me and I gave up. 'OK,' I said. The doctor walked away to a desk in the corner of the room. I saw her speak to the person behind it. He picked up a phone. Presumably to call an ambulance.

We sat like the disciples in the upper room before the Holy Spirit turned up. Nobody could think of much to say to anyone else. David who, as organiser of the trip, was sort of responsible for me told me he would phone my parents as soon as he was back in England to let them know what had happened and that I was in safe hands. Yes, he said in response to my query, he had my parents' number on file. 'Trust me,' he said. Then he gave me a really rather lovely smile and squeezed my hand by way of reassurance. Dickon kept looking at me with anguish in his face. I know that he would have started crying if he'd tried to speak. The minutes were ticking by towards the moment when the bus had to leave for the airport. Would the ambulance arrive before that moment, or would my companions and Natasha have to leave me alone in the station waiting room, hoping for the best? In the end it all happened at once. Natasha finally said, 'We must go now,' in a very distraught voice, but at the same moment the ambulance turned into the yard and came to a stop right outside the door. Natasha and Dickon between them helped me into it.

'Phone number,' Dickon said.

'No pen, no paper,' I said. 'They're in my case. In the bus.'

'Same here,' said Dickon. But he went on. 'I'll find you. I'll find you through Jenny, or through David. I'll come to Durham.'

'You're lovely,' I said. I was lying in the back of the

119

ambulance. Dickon was outside, separated from me by the length of my body. We were too far apart to kiss or touch properly. Though he did momentarily squeeze one of my feet. He looked overwrought. He turned away then, unable to speak, and walked with the others towards the bus. The rear hatch of the ambulance was banged shut.

It was the kind of ambulance that is like a hatchback saloon car rather than a high-sided van. I lay in it on my back like a corpse in a hearse; the difference was that I could see out. I could see upwards. I could see the trolley-bus wires as we passed beneath. I could see the tops of the buildings that lined the streets. I could see the tops of the trees ... and I registered with surprise that they were beginning to break bud and come into leaf. I'd been four hundred miles north of Moscow for a whole week. I'd had a sense of spring arriving during our last two days in Leningrad – and in particular at Novgorod. Down here it was several days more advanced.

I saw all this: the trees, the building tops. But I had no idea which parts of Moscow we were travelling through. Despite the sunshine I failed to keep track of which direction we were travelling in (we turned and turned again at the corners of every street) and I had no idea where our destination was.

At last we stopped. I hadn't been alone in the taxi with the driver. A woman had been sitting alongside him in the passenger seat. Now the two of them helped me out of the ambulance and stood me on my unsteady feet. Then the taxi drove off. I looked about me. Instead of the front doors or Casualty entrance of a hospital that I expected to see I was confronted with a row of shabby prefabricated huts. I was standing with my female guardian or captor (who spoke no English) on the kind of roadway lined by small trees that runs around housing estates. We walked towards the nearest hut – it was just a few yards across a patch of bare earth on which a tree stood – and my woman knocked with her bare knuckles at a door from which the paint was peeling off. The windows nearby were barred, I noticed. I was reminded of ciné footage I had seen of concentration camps.

Nobody answered the knock. The buildings in front of us were so silent and looked so untenanted that I couldn't believe anybody ever would. My companion knocked a second time. And after a decent interval a third. At last, almost to my disbelief, there came the sound of bolts being drawn back and the door being unlocked. The door opened. A nurse stood in the doorway. The featureless space behind her was brightly lit. She welcomed me in with a gesture made with her arms but no smile accompanied it. The other woman stayed outside; the door was shut on her and locked, and she disappeared from my life.

I was in what seemed more like a bathroom with a bed in it than any hospital room I'd seen before in my life. To the left of the street door was the toilet bowl, to the right the washbasin and bath. Directly ahead was another, internal, door with frosted glass in its panels. Next to it was the iron bed. The nurse did a mime to indicate that I should get undressed and get into it. Then she left through the internal door, and I heard the sound of her turning the key in its lock.

Laid out on the bed were pyjamas. They were the only fun thing about the place. They were a double set. There was an inside pair, of navy blue cotton, and an outer pair that comprised jacket and trousers of navy blue corduroy, decorated with a pattern of gold stars like the dome of the monastery at Suzdal. I put both pairs on and got into bed.

Perhaps half an hour passed. A woman doctor in a starched white coat came in with a glass of water and pills for me to take. She didn't speak English. Trustingly I swallowed the pills she held out. She left. I heard the sound of the door being locked again as soon as she was the other side of it.

A little later I got out of bed to have a pee – it was just three paces across the room to where the toilet bowl was – and noticed that there was no loo paper. Not that I needed it right now. But I would at some point. With my lack of Russian and everyone else's lack of English this might become a difficult issue to sort out. For now, though, I climbed back into bed.

Lunch came eventually. It was a plate of meatballs accompanied by a small mound of boiled buckwheat. Somehow I ate it.

It was during that long afternoon that the completeness of my isolation came home to me, bit by bit. I could phone nobody outside this hospital – if indeed a hospital was what it was. I could speak to nobody inside the place. My suitcase had gone off in the bus to the airport. I had no books, no pen or paper, no toothbrush, no toothpaste, no deodorant. Most of what I was, most of who I was, was somewhere else.

I tried to remember what time the flight had been due to leave. I tried to work out whether it would have landed at London Heathrow yet. What time would it be in England? I had difficulty sorting this out. Perhaps my high fever was affecting my capacity to do elementary arithmetic. (Not that arithmetic had ever been my strongest suit.) My reason for trying to think about all this was simple. I wanted to know where Dickon was. At the airport? On his train back down to Exeter? Already at home with his parents? What was he doing? What was he thinking about? Was he thinking about me? Was he worrying about what had happened to me? I was sure he was.

On my own in an unfamiliar bed in a place whose name I didn't know – I wasn't even quite sure of its purpose – with nothing of my own about me except the day clothes I had earlier taken off, I wanted Dickon as thirstily, as hungrily, as I'd wanted anything or anyone in all my life. I was determined not to start crying about this. But my determination proved insufficient. Eventually I felt the chill of tears cooling as they ran down my cheeks. I realised that I'd left my handkerchief in my trouser pocket. And the trousers, along with my other clothes, had been taken somewhere else. I couldn't even mop my tears up easily. I made do with the corner of the sheet.

Someone arrived some time later to tidy the room a bit. She spoke a lot of Russian at me. I tried to explain that I didn't speak the language. I knew that *Nyet* was 'No'... Everybody knew that. And when I'd heard the idea of 'Russian' expressed as an adjective it had sounded like *po Rooskie*, or something like that. So I tried, *'Nyet po Rooskie.'*

It obviously wasn't quite what I'd meant. The woman echoed, *'Nyet po Rooskie!!'* then repeated it a second time, in a tone of utter contempt and disbelief. Had I told the woman her mother was a whore she could not have replied with more outrage in her voice.

But I couldn't let the woman just go about her business in offended silence. I needed to explain about the lack of toilet paper while I had the chance. I hauled myself half out of the bed, turned my bum towards the woman and made an arse-wiping gesture across the seat of my gold-spangled corduroy pyjamas with my wrist.

If the woman had been horrified by my attempt at vocal communication, my mime rendered her nearly apoplectic. I pointed a jabbing finger at the empty loo-roll holder with all the urgency I could summon in my weakened state. At last she saw what I was pointing at and got the message. She left the room a moment later, locking the door after her carefully as she went. A minute later she was back, to my immense relief, with a couple of rolls of bumf. She installed one of them in the holder and placed the other one upright on the top of the cistern by way of back-up. I smiled gratefully at her. She didn't return the smile, but at least I'd achieved the object I'd been after. I had learnt how to communicate.

It grew dark outside the un-curtained window. Someone came with more pills for me to take. Someone brought my supper. It was meatballs and boiled buckwheat, exactly the same as it had been at lunch.

Soon after I had eaten I heard the sound of the interior door being once again unlocked. Somebody was ushered into the room by another, unseen someone – who locked the door again as soon as the visitor was on my side of it. I stared at my visitor – my apparition – in astonishment and happy wonder. It was Natasha. With a jar of preserved peaches and a tin of apple slices. And a smile on her face.

It was only with an enormous effort that I refrained from crying again. 'Oh Natasha,' I said. I wanted to hug her to me. At that moment I loved Natasha as dearly as I loved my mother. 'Oh Natasha.'

'It's all right Oliver,' Natasha said. 'You are in safe hands. You are going to be looked after. Already your temperature is coming down a bit, they said.'

'They?' I asked. 'Who are they? Where am I? What is this place?'

'Don't be afraid, Oliver.' Natasha grinned encouragement. 'You are in the Botkin Hospital. It's one of the biggest hospitals in Moscow and one of the best. It has two thousand inmates. You are in the isolation unit.'

'And where is it?' I went on. 'In relation to the centre, I mean. North? South? East...?'

'More or less,' Natasha said.

'Natasha,' I said. 'I have no luggage with me. I have no books to read. How long will I be here? I have no toothbrush and no toothpaste. What illness have I got?'

'You have measles, Oliver,' Natasha said. 'My boss has telephoned the British Embassy and they have contacted the Consulate. From there they will send you books. Also, now that you ask, some toothpaste and a toothbrush...'

'I have to apply to the Consulate for toothpaste and a brush...?'

'They will come soon. Tomorrow, I am sure.'

'Will you come again tomorrow, Natasha...?' I heard the desperation, the beseeching, the begging tone in my voice.'

'Oh Oliver I am very sorry. Tonight I must go back to Leningrad with another group of students for a week.'

'A week? Will I still be in here when you get back?'

'I can not say that. The doctors have told me they will keep you here for about one week. Maybe a little longer, maybe a little less. I may see you again before you go home to England. Or I may not.'

I was torn. I wanted to be out of this place before the week was up. But I didn't want to leave without seeing Natasha again. For this brief extraordinary moment she was the most important and the loveliest person in my life.

'If I am not here there will be someone else. A colleague of mine called Sveta. She will keep in touch with you. She will come and see you. She will arrange the toothpaste and the toothbrush. Talk with the Consulate about books... Oh wait. I nearly forgot something very important. I have a written note for you. Written by Dickon and Jenny on the bus to the airport. They gave it to me to give to you.'

Natasha reached into her large utilitarian handbag and fished out a scrap of paper. It was the flimsiest piece of paper you could imagine, but at that moment the most important object in my shrunk universe. Natasha handed me the paper. It was the centre-fold page from a pocket diary – a diary that must have been in the smallest size that diaries come in: the paper, when unfolded, covered roughly the same area as a book of stamps. I read what was written on it with a desperate eagerness, while Natasha politely stood beside the bed.

TWELVE

On the tiny page intended for engagements on June 13th 1986 was written:

Dear Oliver

A note written on a piece of diary paper on a bouncing Russian bus isn't much comfort but we're all thinking of you. Get well soon & see you in Durham.

Lots of love

Jenny

While on June 14th's page was:

Cher Oli

What can I say? Really shocked by this turn of events and downhearted not to be travelling with you. I'll find you again. Durham soon or Edinburgh.

Love and Kisses

Dick

I stared at the open double-page for several seconds after I'd finished reading. I could vividly picture Dick and Jenny sitting next to each other as they bounced over the potholes, scrounging this flimsy scrap of paper from someone, and inevitably reading over each other's shoulders as they awkwardly wrote. Dick had written Love and Kisses. I felt the smart of tears in my eyes. I remembered that Natasha was standing silently two feet away.

'Thank you, Natasha,' I said. 'Thank you for bringing me this.'

'It is important, I know,' Natasha said and smiled.

'But you are going away,' I said. 'I'll miss you.'

'You will soon be well again. Then you will be back in England and you will see your friends. Especially Jenny. Especially Dickon too.' She smiled again. 'I know.'

We chatted for a minute or two more, then Natasha, still standing because there was no chair in the room, and still in her overcoat, said that she had to go. She pressed a bell near the door – it had been pointed out to me when I first arrived but I'd forgotten it – and after a further minute someone came to let her out. Natasha turned back to me for one last second. She took my hand and squeezed it. 'Be brave,' she said. Then she was gone.

I lay back on my pillow, reliving the whole experience of Natasha's visit in my mind – in my impressionable state it had taken on an aura of the supernatural, almost the miraculous – and wondering if I would ever see Natasha again. Then I re-read the precious mini-missives that I still held in my hands.

Later that evening, when I was drowsy with pills and fever, I heard a sort of distant chanting: a female voice in some corridor far away; I remembered the chanting women we had heard and seen in the monastery at Zagorsk. But this here-and-now chanting grew nearer and I was astonished to find that I could make out the words, and that I knew what they meant. *Chay i smetana.* Tea and sour cream. I couldn't see what was happening in the corridor outside but I found that my other senses were compensating – as I knew was the case for people who went blind – for what I couldn't see. I became aware, through the faint sounds of wheels and rattling, of opening and shutting doors, that a trolley was being pushed along. And sure enough, my own door opened eventually and the bedtime drinks arrived. One glass of steaming tea, one smaller glass of sour cream. The cream was thin enough to drink without a spoon; it had the consistency of Milk of Magnesia. The tea was accompanied by the familiar, cement-solid, cube of sugar. Both drinks were welcome and wonderful. I realised as I savoured them that for the next week this before-sleep moment would probably be the highlight of my day.

In the morning I read my two letters twice before breakfast, which was porridge made from buckwheat. I discovered that the morning sun played up and down the trunk of the chestnut tree outside my barred window. It reached a certain point, recognisable because a branch had been sawn off there, just after ten o'clock. At that moment I allowed myself to read my letters again. I knew that I would need to ration myself, or they would grow stale and meaningless. I read them again just before lunch (which was meatballs and boiled buckwheat) and then again afterwards.

Dear Oliver

A note written on a piece of diary paper on a bouncing Russian bus isn't much comfort but we're all thinking of you. Get well soon & see you in Durham.

Lots of love

Jenny

And,

Cher Oli

What can I say? Really shocked by this turn of events and downhearted not to be travelling with you. I'll find you again. Durham soon or Edinburgh.

Love and Kisses

Dick

My eyes lingered especially on the last word but three of that second letter. Love. People wrote that word in letters. Even one or two of my old school-friends did when we exchanged letters these days. But still... I touched the word with my finger. I ran the tip of my finger over it, trying to feel the indentation the biro had made in the paper against my fingerprint.

Afternoon brought tea and pills. I pointed out the jar of peaches and the un-opened tin of apples that stood on my bedside locker. I could have opened the peach jar easily, but not the tin of apples. And eating fruit in syrup without a spoon or plate would have been a messy business as well as difficult.

Happily my gestures were understood. The nurse or orderly came back with a spoon, a dessert plate and a tin-opener of the old-fashioned sort that resembles a dagger as much as anything else. At least, if I had an accident with it I was in the right place, I thought.

I paid a visit to my bedside toilet. Here I made a discovery. Sitting on the loo seat and peering up at the frosted glass internal window beside and above it I could see that there was a patch of glass in the window pane, little bigger than a large coin, where the frosting, which must have been an applied coating, had come off. Through this spy-hole I could clearly see the folded hands of the patient in the room next to mine. They were at rest, on the top of the bed covers. They belonged, I guessed, to a woman who was elderly. I had a neighbour! The feeling this discovery gave me was unexpectedly intense.

I re-read my letters before dinner by way of an aperitif. Dinner was meatballs and boiled buckwheat. I read the letters again afterwards. Then I lay still, waiting, almost counting down the minutes, till the faint cry of *chay i smetana* could be heard in the far distance. It grew louder, grew nearer, and at last the trolley entered the room. Gratefully I took my bedroom drinks and imbibed them. At last I drifted off into sleep.

The following day, when it arrived, was an identical copy of the one described above.

There were a few minor differences. A very large spider appeared from nowhere and sat patiently in the bottom of the bath. Its condition resembled mine, I thought. Its state of mind too, most probably.

And when I looked through my spy-hole in the frosted glass above the loo seat I saw the hands of my elderly woman neighbour doing something amazing. They were peeling a pineapple. With a knife. Upon a plate. A whole pineapple. Where in all Moscow had someone managed to find that?! A whole pineapple. For one elderly lady. She'd never get through it. All by herself... I had to remind myself that I still had a half-full jar of peaches and half a tin of apples beside my bed. I should be grateful for what I had.

The other thing that happened was that I dropped my watch on the hard tiled floor when I was looking at it at ten o'clock. I was checking to see whether it was time for me to re-read Dickon's note or not. It was. I was pleased about that. But the watch slipped out of my hand. I'd been keeping it on my bedside table, along with the apples and peaches; I didn't wear it while I was in bed the way Dickon did. The watch still said ten o'clock when I picked it up. But it went on saying ten o'clock. I was afraid I might cry again about that – but I did not. I could still tell the time, although only approximately, from the slow movement of the sunlight up and down the tree trunk.

The day ended as the previous two had. The cry of *chay i smetana* was heard in the corridor. It came like an evening prayer or blessing. I drank my tea and sour cream and found a surprising feeling of peace. I wondered if this was something that monks felt at the ends of their days of thought and silence. I wondered if the feeling was shared by the spider at the bottom of my bath. Whom I had now christened Bruce.

In the morning breakfast was not buckwheat porridge for once. It was rice pudding instead.

'Good morning, Oliver.'

I must have been dozing. I hadn't heard the door unlocked or opened. I looked up at my visitor in astonishment. Not only had I been greeted in English. My visitor was male. I hadn't seen a male human being for three days. My ambulance driver had been the last; Dickon the one before that. 'Good morning,' I said.

The man who stood before me was a doctor. He wore a stethoscope and a white coat. He looked about thirty and his looks were good. I didn't normally consider men good-looking if they were older than about twenty-two. But there are exceptions to every rule and, besides, I hadn't seen a man of any sort for half a week.

'They told me,' said my visitor, 'that there was a young man from England who nobody could talk to and who could talk to no-one. I thought I should come and say hallo at least.'

'That's very kind of you,' I said. 'Hallo.'

'Hallo.' My visitor smiled, a bit tentatively.

'How did you know my name was Oliver?'

'It is written on your door. On the side of the door you can not see.'

'Thank you for coming,' I said. What I wanted to do was to throw my arms around him, topple him onto the bed and squeeze him till he couldn't breathe. Then I realised I had an urgent question. 'What's your name?'

'Dmitri,' he said. He said it shyly, as though sharing something deeply personal. 'Or Doctor Stepanov. But I'm not your doctor. Not officially. So please call me Dmitri.'

'Thank you Dmitri,' I said. He had arrived as though winched down from a helicopter to someone adrift on a horizonless sea. His name was the only thing – the precious tenuous thread – that connected us. It was the only thing I would be able to cling to if he were equally suddenly to be winched away. I said – I heard the diffidence in my voice as I spoke – 'Would you sit down with me?'

I shifted my legs sideways to make room for him and he sat down in the space I'd provided for him alongside my knees. I had the feeling I had when a cat unexpectedly sought my company or a bird alighted to feed for the first time from my outstretched hand. I said, 'I haven't spoken English for three days.'

Dmitri said, 'And I haven't spoken English for three years. You will have to forgive my lack of...'

'Please don't apologise,' I said. 'I'm just so grateful that you're here. Thank you for...' I stopped. If I went on saying thank you to him every time I opened my mouth he would become so exasperated that he would leave.

'Where do you live in England?' he asked me.

'I live in a village near Canterbury in Kent,' I said. 'I don't know if you know...'

'Canterbury is very important in history,' Dmitri said, nodding. 'It is England's principal religious town. It is between London and the sea that separates England from France. Is that right?'

'Well done,' I said.

'Saint Augustine and the Archbishop of Canterbury...'

'You're very well ... informed. Have you been to England?'

'Alas no,' said Dmitri. 'I know England – and Britain – from books only. But maybe one day.'

'You must come and be my guest,' I said. It was such an easy thing to say. I knew as well as Dmitri did that there was not the remotest chance of the invitation being taken up.

Dmitri looked around my bedside. I could see him take in the tin and jar of fruit and the spoon and plate that went with them. 'Have you got everything you need?' he asked. Then without stopping, 'Are those things clean?'

'The spoon and plate? They were replaced this morning. I haven't used them yet. The people here are very good about that.'

'Good,' said Dmitri. 'What about other things?' I must have given him an odd look. 'Other things you might need during your stay. I thought books maybe...'

'Books in English are on their way from the consulate or the embassy. They just haven't yet arrived. But one thing I haven't got – it's actually two things – is toothpaste and a brush to clean my teeth.'

'Oh dear,' said Dmitri. 'I shall see what I can do. Maybe later today. But tomorrow certainly.'

'Thank you,' I said. It just slipped out of me.

'I shall not ask you if you are enjoying the food.' Dmitri gave me a smile that was collusive, conspiratorial.

'It is different,' I said diplomatically.

'They do their best,' Dmitri said.

I nodded. I understood, of course, that costs had to be kept down. And then an alarming thought struck me. I voiced it immediately. 'It must be costing a lot to keep me here. Will I ... will my parents ... be getting an enormous bill?'

Dmitri shook his head and smiled reassuringly. 'Do not worry,' he said. 'There will be no bill. There is an arrangement between the Russian health service and yours. It is the same for Russian citizens who are taken ill while visiting the UK. There is nothing to pay on either side. It is ... how do you say it? ... re... recip...'

'Reciprocal,' I supplied. A tide of relief floated the word. 'Thank you. Thank you.'

Dmitri moved his hand a few inches across the bed cover and tweaked my knee. Then he smiled at me.

THIRTEEN

The following morning I was presented with a telex message. It read: *Tried to phone hospital. See you soon I hope. Love Mother.*

I'd never had a telex message before. They were mostly used in business. My mother must have had to go to the village post office to send it. I could picture her there, dealing with this unfamiliar method of communication, helped by the counter clerk. Like the telegrams that people used to use in emergencies when I was a child.

So she had tried to phone the hospital. Poor Mum! But with my father by her side, I hoped, at least. I could picture her gamely trying to speak in English to the hospital's switchboard till the phone was put down in exasperation at the Russian end.

I couldn't reply to the message of course. But at least I knew now that my parents knew where I was; I knew that David Cotton had managed to get in touch with them. And I now had something else to read.

To

Dear Oliver

A note written on a piece of diary paper on a bouncing Russian bus isn't much comfort but we're all thinking of you. Get well soon & see you in Durham.

Lots of love

Jenny

and

Cher Oli

What can I say? Really shocked by this turn of events and downhearted not to be travelling with you. I'll find you again. Durham soon or Edinburgh.

Love and Kisses

Dick

was now added

Tried to phone hospital. See you soon I hope. Love Mother.

My morale increased enormously as a result. I was learning that when words really matter it is not the number of them that counts.

But my morale was already on the up thanks to Dmitri's visit. He had stayed with me for over twenty minutes – during which time, I presumed, he should really have been dealing with his own patients somewhere else. During those twenty minutes he had tweaked my knee three times and I had touched the sleeve of his white coat once. After he departed from my room (there was some reluctance displayed on both sides at that moment) I lay back down on my pillow with a wonderful feeling of elation – almost of inflation – inside me, as though I had just knocked back a large whisky or inhaled deeply on a spliff.

That next day, the day of my mother's telex, Dmitri came again in the afternoon.

In the intervening twenty-three hours I had conjured his face almost as often as I'd conjured Dickon's. In my mind I had seen his form, replayed his movements, recreated the way he moved; I'd felt the weight of him sitting on the edge of my bed and – inevitably – those three tweaks of my knee. I'd wondered about him. What was his home life like? The home life of any Russian was difficult for me to imagine. I couldn't imagine Natasha's for instance. Still less could I picture Dmitri's. Did he still live with his parents? Share a flat with other young doctors? Was he married? Did he have small children already? Did he and his young family have an apartment of their own? Now, at approximately three o'clock in the afternoon, as measured by the sun on the tree trunk outside, here he was again.

Because I had called his features to mind so

141

constantly since his first visit they had inevitably changed somewhat, as though worn with use. The reality now in front of me was slightly different. Yet this was the real Dmitri. His imagined face faded quickly from my mind. I wondered for a quick second whether the same thing would happen when I saw Dickon again; I'd conjured his face before me even more often than Dmitri's after all. But I put this thought behind me as well. I had my current visitor to focus on. 'Hallo again,' I said. 'Take a seat.' I moved my legs aside to make room for him, just as I'd done the day before. But this time I didn't move them quite so far.

'*Spassibo,*' he said as he took his seat on the bed. I had told him yesterday that I knew the Russian word for thank you. As he pronounced it now he looked at me with a very bright twinkle in his blue eyes. 'You're looking better today. That is as it should be. Now I have something for you.' He fished in the pocket of his white coat and produced a small paper bag that was furled into a nearly tubular shape. He handed it to me.

I opened the bag. Inside were a tube of toothpaste and a toothbrush to go with it. I remembered how Michael – Doctor Peters – had managed to run a tube of toothpaste to earth in GUM, and that it hadn't been a particularly easy thing. I said thank you. '*Spassibo.*' I touched the sleeve of his coat and for a second awkwardly rubbed his forearm. He smiled at that and didn't flinch away.

I saw him looking at my bedside locker. 'You are eating your fruit,' he said. 'That is good.'

'It is very nice,' I said. 'But I'm not sure how much vitamin C is left in fruit after it's bottled or canned.'

'About thirty-three percent if I remember,' Dmitri said. 'But it's better than nothing.'

'I agree,' I said, though up till then I probably hadn't done.

'And we are still only in April. The season of fresh fruit – even the beginning of it – is a month or two away.'

'Two days ago I saw the lady in the next room eating a whole pineapple. A fresh pineapple. At least I saw her peeling it.' I felt I needed to explain. 'There's a piece of glass in the window over there that isn't frosted. I can just see her hands through it if she's lying in bed.'

I suddenly saw that Dmitri's face had fallen and at the same moment realised why. He said, 'I'm not sure where I could find you a pineapple...'

'Oh Dmitri,' I said, dismayed. 'I didn't mean... I wasn't trying to...' I clasped his nearer hand. He didn't say anything but with his other hand clasped the other one of mine. For some seconds we stayed like that, gazing into each other's eyes, neither of us knowing quite what to say.

Then Dmitri let my hand go and I released his a half second later. 'You still have no books, I see,' Dmitri said.

'I know. The Embassy – or the Consulate – seem to have… Natasha did say she'd contacted them.'

'Natasha?'

'She was our tour guide,' I said. 'She's very kind. She came back to see me the evening I came in here, even though she had to go to Leningrad that night on the sleeper train. Are you married, Dmitri?'

I didn't know where that question had suddenly popped out from.

'No,' he said then, very soberly, 'Do you have a girlfriend in England, Oliver?'

'No,' I said. I found I wanted to tell him all about Dickon, and about Mo, and about how confusing life was, but I realised I couldn't. One reason was that my thoughts were in too much of a tangle to put them into words, another was that it would take all day. Instead I repeated, 'No,' and heard it sounding horribly final, like the repeated tolling of a funeral bell.

'How old are you?' Dmitri asked.

'Nineteen,' I said.

'Then you have plenty of time to find a girl.' He chuckled. 'Don't worry. You have everything ahead of you.'

I said, 'I don't think I want to find a girl.' Maybe that was my shorthand way of telling him about Dickon and about Mo and about how   confusing life was.

144

Dmitri was silent for a moment. Then he said, 'Perhaps it is the same for me.'

It was my turn to be silent for a second. Then I asked, 'Do you live at home with your parents ... or ...?'

'My parents live in the Ukraine. In a town called Pripyat. You will not have heard of it. I live near here, in an apartment that belongs to the hospital. I share with other young doctors. We are six.' He smiled. 'It is quite.... How do you say...?'

'Cramped?' I suggested. 'Cosy? Quite fun?'

'Yes,' Dmitri said, smiling. 'It is all of those.' And at that point he laid his hand on my knee. He didn't tweak it this time. Just put his hand over it and kept it there.

'I wish I could come there,' I said. 'Come and visit you at home, I mean. Meet your friends.'

Dmitri laughed. 'That might be difficult in the state you are now. In those clothes...' I felt his hand rub my knee.

I laughed too. 'I meant when I'm better.'

'Even that might not be so easy. It isn't easy for western people to go into private houses and apartments here. You probably know that already.'

I said, 'I do. I was probably just joking really.'

'Probably,' said Dmitri, and I heard a kind of sadness in his voice that I struggled to understand.

'You mentioned my clothes,' I said. 'What do you think of them?'

'I don't know what you call that material…'

'Corduroy.'

'The gold stars on the dark blue…'

'Like the dome on the monastery in Suzdal,' I said – and immediately thought of Dickon.

'You're funny,' he said.

'How's my temperature today?' I asked.

'I do not have your chart,' he said. 'And I have no thermometer in my pocket. You are not my patient, after all.' He leaned forward and placed his hand on my forehead.

'That feels nice,' I said. 'The touch of a human hand.'

He didn't take the hand away as he said, 'You still have a fever but it is not so very high. I would guess it is coming down. In a few days you will be at home.' Then he did remove his hand from my forehead and slowly sat back up, but his other hand gave a little stroke to my leg just above the knee.

I said, 'That's nice too.'

He didn't say anything to that but his massaging of my upper leg grew slightly bolder and more confident. He looked searchingly into my eyes. I smiled up at him.

He said, 'Are you OK?'

I understood him perfectly. I nodded happily and his hand explored a little further up my thigh. I said, 'You're very nice, Dmitri.'

He said, 'You're beautiful.'

I said, 'Go on.'

His hand moved slowly up my leg. Almost as slowly, I thought, as the sun moved up the trunk of the tree outside. It reached the point where the back of it brushed against my balls. 'Ah,' he said, 'what have we here?'

'You're a doctor,' I said cheekily. 'You should know.'

We both giggled at that moment and I felt him grab my cock through the blankets. Only now that he was holding it did I know what state it was in physically. Partly stiff but very small. I felt I had to explain. 'It's usually bigger than that. It's being ill, and what with the pills they're giving me...'

'You don't have to explain,' Dmitri said very softly. 'I know. It's very nice anyway.'

I said throatily, 'Under the covers. Put your hand down inside...'

Dmitri stood up and moved close to my shoulders and head. He glanced quickly at the frosted glass of the interior door. Then he put his hand on my cheek and caressed it, then ran it down over my collar bone and down beneath the turned-back sheet. As he moved his hand down, it very expertly undid the buttons of my corduroy top, but it could do nothing about the vest-type under-pyjama-top beneath. Until it got to the hem at the bottom at which point I felt the joy in his finger-ends as they encountered my skin.

I was enjoying it too. Enjoying his exploration of my navel with a fingertip, enjoying his stroking of my pubes. And then the feel of his whole hand grasping my penis, which had managed to get a bit bigger by now. At that moment I reached out towards his crotch – it was just above my shoulder, and his upper legs were pressed hard against the mattress and bed-frame beneath me – and, diving between the flaps of his white coat (which wasn't buttoned, happily) I grabbed his own dick through the fabric of his trousers.

It was huge. At least it was very thick at the base. It might not have been quite as long as Dickon's but it was certainly as long as mine. And the girth of it! It seemed to have about twice the circumference of Dickon's or mine. I wrapped as much of my hand around it as I could manage in those trousered circumstances. And then we both stopped. We looked at each other very seriously, awed by the sudden new situation, by the turn things had taken.

'I have to go,' Dmitri said. His voice was an apologetic mumble. 'I'm sorry. But we can't continue this now. Not here.'

'Of course,' I said. I knew enough to realise that if anyone were to come in and catch us, or even if someone made out our silhouettes through the frosted glass and made four from two and two Dmitri would be out on his ear. Being struck off the medical register in England had consequences enough. I could only imagine what it might involve here.

Slowly Dmitri released my cock and let his hand travel back up my body beneath the sheet the way it had come. Equally slowly I released his massive hard-on and allowed my hand to trail down the front of his thigh until the point where it was pressed hard against the bed and I couldn't follow it any more. Dmitri's hand re-emerged above the bedclothes. For the second time he brushed my cheek with it. 'You'll have to do the buttons back up yourself,' he said. 'Sorry.'

'That's OK,' I said. And gently we let each other go.

'I'll come back again as soon as I can,' he said. Reaching down he tweaked my knee.

'I'll look forward to that,' I said.

Then Dmitri fished in his pocket for a big bunch of keys and let himself out of my presence, disappearing like the sparrow that flies through the feasting hall into the who knew where.

FOURTEEN

Dmitri's visit hadn't brought me anything more to read. But it had given me a hell of a lot to think about. As I read Dickon's note for the umpteenth time I was forced to confront what had happened – between Dickon and me, between Dmitri and me – and try to make sense of it. Try, in addition, to reconcile it with my conscience.

Dickon and I had made no promises to each other. Except that Dickon had promised to track me down once I was back in England. We had never said we loved each other. Except that Dickon had written *Love and Kisses* at the end of his note...

But everyone did that these days. Jenny had written *love* at the end of her note and, fond of Jenny though I was, there was no question of love between us. Yes, but Jenny had written *love*. Dickon had written *Love*. He had not written *kisses* but *Kisses*. Those things mattered. His missive comprised a mere thirty-three words, I had to wring every drop of meaning from them. I began to see why generations of people who had nothing else to read had over-interpreted, over-analysed, books like the Bible and the Koran.

So did the *Love and Kisses* forbid me from groping another man's cock through his trousers? And it had only been *through his trousers*. Did it forbid me from inviting another man to reach down into my bed and wrap his fingers round my own member? There was no mitigating circumstance here. No *only through trousers*. Dmitri had begun by grabbing my dick through the sheets and blankets. I had expressly invited him to go further, inviting him to clasp the hot skin of my penis with his warm fingers.

I tried to imagine... What if...? What if Dickon had, in the last few days, played with another guy's cock? If he'd let the other guy touch him? If the circumstances had been more favourable than a hospital bed and they'd gone on and spunked together? If they'd done more than that...? I couldn't go on and imagine any further. The idea of Dickon fucking another man or being fucked by him was altogether too distressing. Even the idea of him touching another man, the idea of him even wanting to...

This gave me a pretty good insight into what Dickon might feel if he knew what I'd done – even the little I'd done – with Dmitri.

I'd suggested – good heavens! – that I'd like to go home with Dmitri and meet his flat-mates. Presumably I'd imagined that, once at his apartment, we'd be able to have a private moment, a private space, and have sex, go to bed, together. As the hours that followed Dmitri's momentous visit passed with lumbering slowness I came to realise that that was the last thing in the world I wanted. What I wanted most, the only thing I wanted, was Dickon. When Dmitri next came to see me I would have to tell him.

After Dmitri left my room I did re-do the buttons of my corduroy pyjamas. I also touched my dick-tip. It was drooling more than copiously, and my pubes were drenching. For a moment I thought I would masturbate but I didn't know what I would do with the resulting ejaculate: I didn't want to leave a map of the whole of the Soviet Union on my very public top sheet or my equally communal pyjamas. So I didn't and, after a while, the desire left me. Perhaps they really did put something in the tea – or the *smetana*.

Quite a lot happened during the morning after that second encounter with Dmitri. Shortly before the sun reached its ten o'clock position on the tree trunk a nurse marched in and told me in a bracing voice that it was bath time. She told me that in Russian, but her mimes were as eloquent as mine were growing these days and I got the message clearly. In my turn I told her, through a mime sequence worthy of Marcel Marceau, that Bruce, the current tenant of the bathtub, would have to be dealt with before we ran the water in.

The nurse peered into the tub, spotted Bruce waiting patiently at the bottom, and took prompt action. She opened the outer door with a key, to my astonishment, and pulled the bolts back, then flung the door open. To my astonishment the mud-patch on the other side of it that I remembered from five days earlier had been transformed by spring grass growth and was a radiant green colour. The small trees across the quiet little roadway were also greening.

My nurse then collared a plastic tumbler from above the wash-basin, pulled out a note book from her breast pocket and then bent down into the bathtub. A second later Bruce was a temporary prisoner, trapped between the tumbler and the notebook. And then he was given his freedom, catapulted – thanks to the wonder of centrifugal force – out into the springtime with one majestic sweep of the nurse's forearm. Then the outside door was shut, bolted and locked again, and my moment's view of the spring-like scene beyond it was withdrawn from me. But it had given me hope. Bruce was my precursor, my advance party. He had had his release from confinement in our miserable shared grey bed/bathroom. He had been given his liberty, and could stretch his eight legs and ramble at will in the insect-busy sunshine. Bruce was my leader. Where Bruce had gone I would soon follow.

I was allowed to take my bath in private. Clean pyjamas were laid out for me by the nurse before she departed. They were russet coloured and patterned. But they were not night-blue, they were not corduroy, they did not have gold stars on them. For all their appearance of clean comfort they were a big disappointment. I wished I could have kept the blue ones. I wondered who would be the next person to get them, after they'd been to the hospital laundry. I hoped he'd deserve and appreciate them.

Bruce was not the only inhabitant of the hospital to get his discharge that day. I noticed when I peered through the clear spot in the window of my toilet area that the bed next door was empty, the woman in it gone, the mattress bare. I wondered, as I briefly bathed, who would take her place, and how soon.

After my bath I wrote a poem. This was no small thing. Partly because I'd never tried to write one before. Partly because until now I hadn't had the means to do so. But the nurse who had run my bath had dropped a pencil on the floor at the moment she'd taken her notebook out of her pocket in order to rescue Bruce. I'd found the pencil later, when I was getting into my clean pyjamas.

As for writing paper, I had the back of the diary page on which Dickon and Jenny had written. There would be room for a very small quantity of autobiographical writing. I would have to watch the number of words and sentences, I realised. I couldn't ramble. I'd have to do it in a very compact format, I thought. It was at that point that I realised it would have to be a poem. Or something in verse form at any rate.

Far from home, far far away,

In prison bathroom painted grey,

They feed me boiled buckwheat, dry bread,

And leave me all day long, alone, in bed.

The Russian nurses always do their duty;

They don't go in much, if at all, for beauty.

Beyond the grimy panes the trees stand bare;

At night no curtains mute the streetlamp's glare.

But day and night the door's shut so I'm locked in

The pride of Moscow's hospitals, the Botkin.

I wrote this sitting up in bed with my knees drawn up towards my chin; I had nothing to press on except the yielding flesh of my upper leg through the blanket, so I had to use the pencil very lightly. I did manage it. But those ten lines filled the available space completely. There was no room to go on and add a verse about Dmitri – or Dickon. Perhaps that was just as well. Thoughts of those two people, and my feelings towards them, already stretched the parameters of what I could make sense of. Trying to express them would have mightily exceeded my capacities as a poet.

After lunch a troop of trainee doctors marched into my small outpost of Britain, led by a senior doctor I hadn't seen before. With them they had a trolley laden with small glasses as if for a drinks party. I was told – by mime, to pull down the top section of my bedcovers and expose my chest. Then a match was struck and a taper lit. The taper was introduced into the glasses one after the other and most of the air expelled from them. The glasses were then placed, upside down, on my chest. They landed with a slight sucking sound and I saw the flesh of my chest mound up a little inside them. I ended up with two rows of them stuck to me, all down my chest, like the teats of a sow. Once they were all in place the doctor and her students departed, locking the door behind them. I had no idea when they might be coming back. Experimentally I rocked my chest to and fro a little. The glasses rocked slightly but did not come loose. They seemed to be stuck as fast as limpets.

At least the team did come back. They pulled the suction glasses off me, but then indicated that I should roll round onto my front. Then they repeated the whole process, with the limpet glasses stuck to my back this time. I resigned myself to my fate a second time. There seemed no point doing otherwise. After all, I was in no pain and I had nothing else to do. I realised then that I was going native. I was acquiring a Russian attitude.

After a time that was un-measurable (with my face pressed down in the pillow I couldn't see the light on the tree trunk) I heard the interior door unlocked and opened. The team were coming back and would release me from my dorsal crest of glass cups. (I imagined by now that I probably looked something like a stegosaurus.) But instead I heard Dmitri's voice. 'Oliver! What are they doing to you? What is going on here?'

'I don't know,' I said stoically. 'I've really no idea.'

'This is ridiculous,' I heard Dmitri say. 'Wait there.' Then I heard him leave the room and lock the door. I thought the instruction to *wait there* was sadly superfluous.

Less than a minute passed before the whole team of doctor and students were back and quickly un-cupping me. They packed up the trolley, pulled my bed covers up, and then left without a word. Seconds later – I had barely had time to roll round onto my back – Dmitri was back in the room.

'Sorry about that,' he said.

'It's OK,' I said. 'But what was that all about?'

'It's an old practice – I think it's called cupping in your language. It's supposed to release toxins from the skin by means of vacuum suction. It is of doubtful efficacy, but it is still taught in the schools… May I sit down?'

'Of course,' I said. 'I'm sorry. I forgot to say…'

He sat in his accustomed position on my bed and looked at me. I looked at him. His face looked anxious for a second or two but then it melted into a confident smile. I realised then that, though he was at least ten years older than me, he was a very handsome guy indeed. 'So how are you today?' he asked, and placed his hand gently on my knee.

'Better now,' I said.

We talked for a while. I told Dmitri the story of Bruce. He wondered why I'd given my ex-room-mate such a name. I told him the story of Robert the Bruce, whose resolve was strengthened by the example of determination and refusal to accept defeat that had been given him by the spider with whom he, like me, had been sharing accommodation that was less than ideal. We talked too of other things. But all the time we were conscious of the memory of what had happened between us last time Dmitri came to see me. Of what we'd done, and what we hadn't done, and what we'd nearly done. It lurked beneath the surface of our interaction just as Bruce had lurked in the depth of the bathtub. It stayed there, holding on to our thoughts and feelings tenaciously and wouldn't go away.

Dmitri's hand began to massage my leg. Below as well as above the knee. He got his hand as far round behind my lower leg as the blankets would allow. 'You have nice calves,' he said.

'Give over,' I said. 'You're flattering me. I've got the skinniest legs you ever saw.' But I was delighted with his compliment all the same. I remembered that Dickon had enjoyed stroking my calves and thighs. Perhaps my legs weren't so bad after all. But I said, 'They're not a patch on yours.' He looked at me a bit uncertainly. 'That means they're not as good as yours.' By now I was sitting forward in the bed, the covers were down to my waist and I was reaching out and stroking Dmitri's calf and thigh.

'I wish I could see you properly,' said Dmitri. I could feel the sexual tension mounting inside him just as it was mounting inside me. 'I wish I could see you without your clothes.'

'I wish I could see you without yours.'

That would not have been possible in the place where we were, unless Dmitri was prepared to spend the night in a police cell. But I did think that his wish would not be completely impossible to grant – with a few limitations. I unbuttoned the outer jacket of my pyjamas and deftly stowed it beneath the pillow. Before Ditri had time to speak I followed suit with the pyjama singlet beneath it. Then I reached down inside the bed and pushed my pyjama bottoms down as far as my knees. There they met the obstruction of Dmitri's hand. He lifted it away for a second and I slid the pyjama trousers halfway down my calves.

Dmitri murmured something. Something like, 'Ooh, ooh.'

I said, 'Lie on top of me, Dmitri.'

He nodded, but he wanted to something else first. After a quick look at the frosted-glass door, checking for silhouettes in the corridor, he pulled the blankets down and took a look at me.

I may have been skinny and un-muscular – my ribs showed individually – but Dmitri clearly liked what he saw. My prick especially. I had been growing stronger day by day, as quickly as a nestling bird, and my cock had kept pace with me. It was now almost as big and stiff as it had used to be before I got ill. Dmitri gave it an affectionate squeeze. Then he wanked it for a second. Just two strokes up and back. Then he undid the waistband of his trousers and the zip below them. Then he lay flat on top of me. I saw his massive cock spring out, and his hefty balls, during the second during which he lowered himself onto me.

He was still glancing constantly across the top of my head to keep a check on the corridor. But in between those glances he was also looking at me. Peering into my eyes, with delight and laughter written in his own. He wriggled his trousers just far enough down so that his cock came into contact with mine. And he pulled his shirt up a little way, so that the warm flesh of his taut belly met the even warmer flesh of mine.

And then it happened. Quite immediately. I had less than two seconds' warning. 'I'm going to come,' I said. By the time I'd finished the sentence I'd already done it. Wetting his belly along with my own.

'Me too,' said Dmitri then. Unexpectedly. I mean I hadn't expected him to ejaculate almost as precipitately as me. He ground his dick against me, thrusting a couple of times, so that I felt it slide creamily up and down the side of my dick, nestled in my groin.

And if I had produced a decent little puddle as, unseeing, I could only suppose, then Dmitri's orgasm was like the sea. He came in wave after wave. I felt his sperm pour out each time in a quantity I'd never experienced before. Not from me. Not from anyone I'd seen ejaculate before. The amount of seminal fluid that he produced and squirted over me was so prodigious that it seemed almost as if he was peeing on me.

When he'd finished coming he lay still for a second.

But a second was all he dared afford. He leaned back off me, doing up his flies, stuffing his wet cock back into his underpants as he did so. 'I'll clean you up immediately,' he said as his feet made hasty contact with the floor. 'Don't move.'

Within a second he'd run to the toilet area and was pulling a yard or more of paper from the roll. A second later he was back at my bedside and, still darting anxious looks through the windowed door, mopping me up – mopping himself up mostly – very expertly. 'Now pull up the blankets quickly,' he told me.

I did. The pyjamas could wait for now. Dmitri returned to the toilet bowl and chucked the wet paper into it. Before flushing he quickly re-opened his flies and gave his own big cock a little clean.

Then he returned to me. More slowly now. He said, 'I don't know what to say…'

I said, 'Thank you, Dmitri. I gave him my hand. He clasped it. Then, after yet one more glance towards the corridor, he leaned down and kissed me.

FIFTEEN

'Chay i smetana, chay i smetana.' The comforting late night chant drifted in from the corridor, down echoing distances that I, having never seen them, could only imagine. Wind-blown distances as vast as the plains that surrounded Vladimir and Suzdal. The windswept plains across which Dickon and I had peered one starry, snowy night. An age ago.

An age ago, a day ago, a night ago, I hadn't had sex with Dmitri. We'd touched each other in a sexual way, certainly, but we hadn't come together. And I'd reminded myself of that constantly as I ran through the whole scenario. Me and Dmitri. Me and Dickon. I'd assuaged my conscience, bolstered myself, with the knowledge that at least we hadn't had actual sex.

Tonight no such comfort was available to me. I had had sex with Dmitri. OK, we hadn't penetrated each other. Hadn't fucked, or swallowed each other's semen. But we had come together; we had pressed our naked cocks together and ejaculated over each other's bellies. A person knows whether he (or she) has had sex with another person or hasn't. Splitting hairs is no help in this. (Yes, but actually we only… Sorry. No.) I had had sex with Dmitri and I knew it. There could be no denying it. Neither to myself nor – if it came to it – to Dickon.

My only comfort tonight was the wonderfully

familiar, safe, cry of *chay i smetana* echoing in the night corridors. And the soothing taste of the two contrasting liquids. The dark clear thin one with its cement cube of sugar, and the thick white one. Though tonight even that was not without unwelcome reminders of the thing that had happened.

I fell asleep eventually. Uneasily. Unhappily. And then... I don't know to this day whether what happened next, what happened in the middle of that night, was real or if I dreamt it. Or if part of it was real and part of it wasn't.

The corridor was full of quiet noise. The sounds of people trying to be quiet but not entirely succeeding. The sounds of people trying to deal with something. Something out of the ordinary. There were hushed voices. There were feet tramping and shuffling. There were wheeled trolleys rolling, their footbrakes softly clamping. There was the sound of frightened people, suffering people, quietly crying.

Then somehow I was in the corridor among them. The corridor stretched endlessly. And all along it ran an endless line of people. People in beds, on stretchers on trolleys, sitting in chairs. There were people with sticks and people with crutches. People swathed in bandages. People whose eyes alone were visible, because their injuries and burns affected every other part of them. People who sat in stoic stillness. People who rocked to and fro, softly keening. People weeping. People moaning. And an endless number of starched and stiff-lipped nurses tending them.

I tried to ask what was happening. I touched the sleeves of nurses, imploring them in Russian to tell me what was going on, what had happened. I might have tried speaking Russian. I might have tried Latin or Ancient Greek. No language would have helped me. For however hard I tried to make my voice work, to make my mouth shut and open, no sound would come out of me, and the nurses brushed me aside, didn't even turn to look at me, but carried on, ignoring me, regardless.

Then suddenly it was morning and the hospital was silent.

The sun rose, as it had to. And breakfast came round, as it had to. But if the orderlies who brought breakfast were usually silent and unsmiling, today they seemed like ghosts, or people who had suffered some awful trauma. I couldn't ask them what had happened. I spoke no Russian.

The day dragged sullenly. The sun crawled snail-like up the grey bark of the tree trunk outside the window. I wished it could travel backwards. I wished it could give me another go at yesterday. I wished that whatever awful thing had come into the world since then could be un-happened.

And as the hours passed painfully, intolerably slowly, I realised that I wanted another thing. I wanted Dmitri.

He didn't come at his usual time in mid-afternoon. I read and re-read my letters from Jenny and Dickon. Especially the one from Dickon.

Cher Oli

What can I say? Really shocked by this turn of events and downhearted not to be travelling with you. I'll find you again. Durham soon or Edinburgh.

Love and Kisses

Dick

That too was painful, in the circumstances. Its tender pathos was almost unbearable. It was I who had made it unbearable. The *Love and Kisses* stung me like a lash of nettles.

What had I done? What had I done to myself? What had I done to Dickon? To me and Dickon? And what awful punishment was I suffering? I felt as if I'd gone to Hell. Gone to Hell and taken the whole hospital – perhaps the whole of Russia – with me.

When supper came I ate a mouthful but nearly choked on it. I left the rest of it.

Then, late on in the evening, my door was unlocked and someone stood in the room with me. Someone in a white coat. He stood still as a statue, unsmiling, looking down at me. It was Dmitri.

'Oh Dmitri,' I said. I burst into tears. I held my arms out towards him. For a moment he hesitated. Then he broke. He leaned down to me and embraced me. I was back in the moments when, as a small child, I had been embraced by my father when I was crying. Dmitri now felt just as solid, just as big and just as powerful. But there was a difference. Dmitri too was crying. As he pressed his cheek against mine I felt the wetness of his tears. And I felt the dismay that anyone experiences at the sound of someone older than himself whimpering.

We just held each other for ages, crying together. Dmitri never looked up towards the door glass to check if anyone was looking. I knew somehow that it no longer mattered if we were caught together. Whatever situation now existed – between Dmitri and me – inside the hospital – in the big world beyond it – was so big and so terrible, that the question of whether Dmitri and I kissed each other, or had sex in my hospital bed, or if we didn't, was no longer of any consequence to anyone.

'Dmitri,' I managed to say at last. 'What has happened? Tell me what has happened.'

I didn't know what I was expecting him to say. But what he did say astonished me. It made no sense to me. I couldn't guess his meaning. 'Pripyat,' he said. 'My parents.'

'Your parents?' I echoed stupidly.

'I don't know where they are,' he said. 'I don't know what has happened to them. I can't find out anything.'

'Dmitri,' I said, as we continued to hold each other, rocking together, like parent and child comforting each other at the bedtime that precedes the start of term. 'What happened here last night? Who were all those people?'

'Nobody knows,' he said. 'Nobody knows except us – the doctors and nurses of Kiev and Moscow. And the brave fire-fighters, the heroic fire-fighters of Pripyat. And the poor, poor people. The workers of Chernobyl. The Russian people know nothing. There is nothing in the newspapers. Nothing on the wireless or the television.'

Pripyat would have meant nothing to me, except that I now remembered Dmitri having mentioned it as the home town of his parents. I had never heard the name Chernobyl. I presumed it was a place near Pripyat.

'An accident?' I hazarded. 'A plane crash? A bomb?'

'An explosion,' Dmitri answered. He was still crying. 'Chernobyl is a place where electricity is generated. How do you call it? The electricity is produced by … uh … dividing atoms.'

I said, 'A nuclear power station.' It all became dizzyingly clear quite suddenly. 'And it is near Pripyat – and your parents live there.'

'My father works there,' he said. 'He worked there. But now I know nothing. All the town of Pripyat has been evacuated. Nobody knows where.'

I had been gazing at my navel. Agonizing about the impact my sexual contacts with Dmitri and my emotional attachment to him would have on my fledgling relationship with Dickon while a catastrophe of world importance had happened and a region of Russia had been devastated – a town had gone up in flames and its people had disappeared to nowhere.

'There were people crying in the corridors during the night,' I said. 'People with...' I didn't know how to go on. The realisation came over me like a wave of nausea. Radiation burns? Radiation sickness? I just about knew the words. I had little idea what they really meant, what they entailed... I realised then that I was starting to worry about myself. Here was Dmitri distraught over the unknown fate of his parents, his country reeling from a tragedy of epic magnitude, and I was thinking about ... me.

I couldn't have really been in the corridor last night, I told myself. That part of my memory of events could only have been a dream. And yet... But I was in an isolation room. The door and walls that protected the rest of the world from me must surely protect me from the rest of the world. Yes, but all I had was a virus. Did radiation work like a virus? Or did it go through walls – like radio waves? You got radiation sickness by handling radioactive things, I remembered vaguely. Or thought I did. Here I was now, cuddling Dmitri, being held by him, in his white coat. Had he been up half the night dealing with radioactive people? Touching them? Now touching me?

He wouldn't be so irresponsible, I told myself. Radioactive people were dealt with by doctors in protective clothing. I'd seen the sort of thing on TV. Yes, but supposing there were thousands of them? Tens of thousands of them? Did any system exist that was big enough to deal with that in any country in the world?

Again I told myself that Dmitri wouldn't be so irresponsible. And then I remembered the sudden and frightening spread of the new disease called AIDS. And I wasn't so sure any more.

'It's all right,' Dmitri whispered to me. 'Don't be frightened. Anyone who was here last night – *if* they were here – would have all been processed and passed through. Nobody who was radioactive would be brought here.'

'And you?' I whispered back.

'I'm safe,' he said. 'You can still touch me. I can still touch you.'

I remembered the conversation Dick and I had had about AIDS before he fucked me.

Then Dmitri surprised me once again. 'I have other news for you, my little friend. Your temperature is down today. Tomorrow you will be released into the world.'

A memory flashed before me like a vision. Of the outside door being opened by a nurse, and Bruce being flung through it into his new life in the green outdoors of the Moscow springtime. I clasped Dmitri tighter to me. I whimpered, 'I don't want to go.'

Another memory came to me, bright and clear as a vision. Night-time conversations with my father, during which he sat on the edge of my bed and held me as Dmitri was holding me now, and I said – the night before the start of every school term in my earliest years

– 'I don't want to go back to school.'

Dmitri said, 'Oh Oliver, my little Oliver, you know you have to go. You can't stay here. You can't stay with me.'

I said, 'I want to live with you.'

He said, 'I want to live with you.' The words came out of him, came from somewhere deep down inside him, like a growl. They were words of pain. Words of despair. The growl of the great Russian Bear.

'I love you,' I said.

'I love you too.'

Those were words I'd only spoken to my parents up till now. They were words that only my parents had spoken to me. Dickon and I hadn't dared to say them – or even to think them – to each other, for fear that in using them we would be casting spells of frightening power that were beyond our control. Now in a moment of extreme emotion and terror of the unknown I'd cast my spell over Dmitri instead, and he had cast his over me. In similar fashion to yesterday, when I had spurted my semen over him, and he had shot his over me.

Then, gently, slowly, Dmitri relaxed his arms and unwound them from me. He repositioned himself on the side of the bed, so that he sat there, facing me, in the same attitude as the one he'd sat in when he first sat down on it an eventful three days ago.

He looked at me gravely, sadly. 'My beautiful little Oliver, I'm sorry. It can not be. It is not possible to live openly as a gay pair in Russia. I can not come to England and live with you. You can not stay in Moscow and live with me.'

'Surely,' I said, 'we can find a way.'

Dmitri sighed, then he smiled bleakly – it was the first thing even approaching a smile that I'd seen him produce this day. 'You are very young and very hopeful. But this is Russia. There is no way. You are a student of history… Go back and read again what you have learnt of Russia's history.'

'Dmitri…'

He placed a finger on my lips very tenderly, silently shushing me. Then he picked up the piece of paper that was my reading matter from my bedside locker and held it in front of me. 'You have people in England who love and care for you. You have Dick. You have mentioned him. Find him again. I can not keep hold of you and you can not keep hold of me. And, anyway, I am too old for you. Your Dick… How old is he?'

Despite the intensity of the moment, despite the primal tragedy of it, I couldn't help smiling as I heard him ask me how old my dick was. As I replied I heard myself answering not only the question he'd thought he was asking but also the one he hadn't. 'The same age as me.'

'You will find him again when you return home, I am

sure. Perhaps you will find happiness with him – who knows? But you are young.' Dmitri shrugged. 'You will find someone. Of that I am sure.'

'Dmitri...' I began, though I had no idea what I wanted to say.

He stood up then. 'Now I have to go.' We looked at each other in silence for a moment. 'You have given me strength,' he said.

I must have given him a look of the most complete astonishment. He almost laughed. 'Believe me.'

Then he leaned down and kissed me and I kissed him and we both cried a bit more. Dmitri stood up straight again. 'I do not think we will meet after today,' he said. 'But we will always be friends in our hearts. I will never forget you.'

'And I will never forget you.' In the last ten seconds I had grown up suddenly. I was no longer a child begging his father not to make him go to school. I was a man who was saying goodbye to someone he would never see again. It happened in life, I knew. I knew that in theory, though. Now I knew it for the first time in my actual experience of the world.

Then Dmitri unlocked the door with his key, passed through it out of my life, and locked it after him.

SIXTEEN

I had come into the hospital in possession of something awful, something that was mine alone: the measles virus. I left the hospital with something much more terrible: a dreadful secret – knowledge of a seismic event that most of Russia did not yet know of.

My arrival at the hospital had taken on a surreal quality as I remembered it. Now equally surreal was the manner of my departure from it.

The British Embassy phoned in the morning. Nobody could tell me they were on the phone, of course, because I understood no Russian. Instead I was instructed by gesture to get out of bed and then ushered through the open internal door into the corridor.

The corridor! I gazed around me, wide-eyed as a toddler who has been taken into Santa's Grotto. The corridor was wonderfully drab – and empty. My mind, my dreams, had filled it with trolleys and stretchers and injured people... Now I felt as though I'd been playing the children's game in which, blindfolded, you step over obstacles and walk round pieces of furniture. Now the blindfold was off and there in front of me ... was nothing.

I was taken into a spartan office. The receiver of the phone on the desk was off the hook and lying on the desk top among a scattering of papers. I was encouraged by gesture to pick the receiver up and speak into it. It was an eerie moment. I guessed that the person on the other end would be my mother or my father. 'Hallo,' I said cautiously. 'This is Oliver Patten.'

'British Embassy, Moscow here,' a male voice astonishingly informed me. 'We've only just had news of your captivity. We'd like to send you some books round…'

I cut the man off. 'That's very kind of you,' I said. 'But actually I'm being discharged some time today and flying back to England.'

'Oh well,' said the voice in a friendly tone, 'that's even better. I'm happy to tell you that flights between Moscow and London are operating normally.' There was a second's silence. 'Just in case you were worried.'

'Thank you,' I said. 'That's good to know.' We said our goodbyes and I put the phone down. *Just in case you were worried,* the man had said. He didn't know what I might know and what I mightn't. He had phrased his sentence, and timed it, most carefully. I realised that diplomats were not so-called for nothing. I was escorted back along the mythic corridor.

By the time I was back in my room my outdoor clothes had reappeared from somewhere. They were laid out on my bed and I was encouraged to get into them. I did so. I paid a farewell visit to the toilet. I looked through my spy-hole. The empty bed next door was no longer empty. A new pair of hands lay on the fold of the new clean covers. The hands were completely swathed in bandages. Even if their owner had had the means to acquire a pineapple they could never have peeled it.

My bowels and bladder emptied, I sat on my bed fully dressed, my overcoat beside me, and waited for something to happen, while the sun moved slowly up the trunk of the tree beyond the window.

I was startled by a ring at the outside door bell. Almost at once a nurse entered from the corridor, crossed my room and unbolted the outside door. She undid the lock, then swung it open. A tall woman in outdoor clothes, with fur hat and big gloves, strode in and greeted me.

'Oliver, I am Sveta. Natasha's colleague. I am so sorry I could not come before. But I was taken ill. Today is my first day back at work. I hope the Embassy has looked after you.'

'They offered to bring me books today,' I said. 'There seems to have been a delay in passing messages to and fro. I told them I was going home.'

'And you are,' said Sveta. 'Only not today. We only just got news of your release and it was not possible to book a flight for today. I am taking you to a hotel. Tomorrow there is a flight for you with British Airways. A taxi will take you to the airport. Come with me.'

It all sounded so normal that it was seriously weird. I got up off the bed and walked with Sveta to the door. Into the room behind us came a bevy of nurses, orderlies, and one of the doctors who had been treating me. They waved me off quite cheerfully, as if they were the cast of an escapist Hollywood musical, and the doctor even smiled at me. Of course Dmitri wasn't among them.

Outside the door a taxi waited. I walked towards it between swards of green grass that smelt of spring. The sun was warm. It was like being in a dream.

Sitting beside Sveta in the back of the taxi I was wafted through the suburbs, then into the centre of Moscow. The streets were full of ordinary people doing ordinary things. Did they know yet, I wondered, about the catastrophe of Chernobyl? Did Sveta know? I could have asked her. I could have told her what I knew. Her English was almost as good as mine. But I held back. It wasn't my job as a visitor from abroad to enquire about such tragic domestic news, let alone break it.

I kept my secret all the way to the hotel. Sveta introduced me to the reception clerk. She told me the times of meals and the time that the taxi would come for me tomorrow. Then she had to go. I took my key and took the lift up to my room.

Inside the room a surprise awaited me. There on the floor stood my suitcase. The suitcase I'd been parted from a week before. I'd last seen it being stowed in the hold of the airport bus. Our reunion was a happy one.

The hotel room was brown. It was clean and drably functional. A window looked down into a street on which people moved. It was my first experience of staying in a hotel alone. It was probably not something that many people got to do at nineteen. I felt unsteady on my feet and rather awed. By myself in the centre of Moscow with only three words of Russian and no way of telling the time, at a moment of national catastrophe.

I was alone with my secret. I was alone with two of them. Not only that there had been a major nuclear disaster some four hundred miles south west of where I was. I also knew that I'd had sex with a man called Dmitri who had lost his parents in the accident; I'd told him that I loved him and he'd said the same to me. I didn't know how to square the first bit of knowledge with the sight of people around me going about their daily lives. I didn't know how to square the second bit with what I felt about Dickon and me. I didn't know what I was going to tell him when I saw him again. I didn't know even if I would see him again.

I knew the expression 'holiday romance'. I knew it as an abstraction only. Holiday romances happened to other people. To people older than me. They weren't good things, I'd always understood, because they never outlived the holiday. I'd never been on holiday without my parents before now. This was my first holiday on my own. It had not been without incident. And I'd gone and had my first holiday romance in the course of it. In fact I seemed to have overdone it a bit. I'd actually had two of them.

I'd seen the time on the clock behind the reception desk downstairs. I guessed that if I spent just a few more minutes gazing down at the street enough time would have passed for it to be lunchtime. So I watched the street life, such as it was, and then went back downstairs.

There were few other people in the dining room. I was shown to a table. I sat. I was served. Sveta had assured me that there was nothing to pay for. The hotel, my food, my re-arranged flight... Insurance covered it all. I ate some lunch, though not very heartily. My normal appetite had not yet returned.

And then I was free. Moscow was mine for the rest of the day. I had a map. The reception desk clerk told me where we were. I headed out to the trolley bus stop and boarded a trolley that was going to Red Square.

The snow had gone. The great square was not very full. Even the queue for Lenin's mausoleum – the queue that we'd joked about, unkindly suggesting it stretched all the way to Vladivostok – seemed shorter than when I'd last seen it. I tramped my way around the vast area. How strange it was to find that in Red Square of all places I should find myself at last surrounded again by familiar things. The red walls of the Kremlin. Their clothes-peg battlements. The ancient gates. The grim-faced guards. How oddly comforting they seemed. How well I seemed to know them.

But I stalked Moscow like a ghost. A ghost who knew things that other Muscovites did not. A ghost who, like Hamlet's father's, had much to tell about the secrets of his prison house but was constrained not to reveal. I could not speak to anyone. No-one could speak to me. Nobody even took any notice of me. I wondered if perhaps no-one could see me, no-one could touch me. That at any moment someone would walk through me as though I were just thin air.

Twice during my stay with the others in Moscow a fortnight ago we had tried to gain entry to the great ice-cream-cone cathedral of St Basil. We had found it shut both times. But today, astonishingly, it was open to the public. I went in.

I knew by now that Russian cathedrals were square. That their cloisters ran round the central core of the building, encasing it, rather than lying along one of its sides as in Western Europe. So I explored its stairways, explored its cloisters and its warm and cosy central space that was full of icons and gold. I grew tired suddenly, as people just discharged from hospital do, and sat down in a convenient chair in a corner of the cloister. One small child saw me and pointed me out to his mother, but she didn't react at all. Perhaps I really was a ghost: an apparition that only a little child could see.

I marched boldly into the foyer of the Metropol Hotel and had a small, hot black coffee. By then I was very tired indeed. I left and headed back to my own, more modest hotel on the crowded trolley bus.

I had dinner early and retired early to my room. I had a book amongst my luggage that I hadn't seen in a long time. The Political Writings of St Augustine that three weeks ago had excited the interest or even suspicion of the Moscow airport Customs. I read a bit of it now. There wasn't much else to do. I had the freedom of the city for the rest of the night if I wanted to take advantage of it. I found that I didn't.

And when I climbed early, wearily, into bed, I found I missed something I'd got fond of in getting used to. The evening chant of *chay i smetana* in a distant corridor, the gentle clatter of the nearing trolley, and the feel on my tongue of the cold sour cream and the hot tea with its insoluble sugar cube.

I stayed in my room that next morning. I didn't dare to venture out in case something happened that might delay me and cause me to miss my appointment with my rescuing taxi. There was a radio in the room, embedded in the furniture. I turned it on a couple of times. A Russian voice was speaking both times. Was the awful news about Chernobyl being delivered now as I listened? Would I hear wails and cries of anguish coming up the stairs? I did not. I picked up one word from the broadcast. It came again and again. The word was *amerikaniski*.

The rescue went like clockwork. My taxi drove me out through the shabby suburbs, past the curtain-less wooden houses, then through forests of pine trees. I arrived for my flight in good time, checked in, went through Customs nervously but successfully, and then sat in the lounge, looking out at the apron and nursing a golden beer. I had a few roubles left. One went on the beer, the others on some plastic souvenirs of Vladimir and Suzdal. I would show them to Dickon. If we ever met again.

A plane slid into view, taxi-ing from an unseen runway. It wore a Union Flag on its tail. BRITISH AIRWAYS was written on it. I was taken aback by the sight of those words. I hadn't seen such uncompromisingly big letters in western script for more than three weeks.

'For anyone who might be worried,' the captain added to his standard welcome on board, 'I can reassure you that we will not be passing anywhere near the disaster area of Chernobyl. Our route takes us well to the north – by some three hundred miles. We will be heading up to the Baltic, crossing the neck of Schleswig-Holstein and then come down the Dutch coast before heading home across the North Sea. No radioactive clouds are anywhere in those vicinities. I wish you a pleasant flight.'

Heading home. Those were the words that hit me.

The first half of the journey was wreathed in cloud. I looked away towards the southern horizon. To where Chernobyl and Pripyat lay in desolate agony, hidden by unheeding clouds of grey. I looked around the aeroplane at my fellow passengers. Were some of them radioactive and didn't know it? Was I? I didn't know enough about anything.

The cloud gave way over Riga and showed us the Baltic Sea, sparkling an unexpected blue. Later, when we'd left Germany behind us, the Friesian Islands appeared like a shark's tooth necklace laid on the water below. The line of them ran westward to a sharp point. We followed it. The line turned south and we did the same. The havens of Holland and Belgium appeared, and in the far distance the White Cliffs of France. Southend Pier. The Thames. The capital city of my country. Windor Castle beneath the wing-tip as we turned... and then we touched home.

My father sounded shaken when I got him on the phone. He hadn't known when to expect me. Had had no news. Except... Had I heard? About Chernobyl? I told him I'd been nowhere near anything radioactive. I was safe and sound. I told him that I knew about Chernobyl but had had no contact with anyone who'd been involved with it. I would be at Canterbury West station in two hours. Children are very careful when it comes to shielding their parents from the worrying things in life.

The doctor told me to take it easy for seven more days. University could survive for a couple of days without me. Just potter about at home, he said. Build my strength up. Don't risk anything else going wrong before my immune system had recovered. Then he looked at me a bit beadily. I hadn't had any contact with anyone who'd been near Chernobyl, had I? In a Moscow hospital...? I said no. Doctors too need protecting from the worrying things in life sometimes.

But I took his advice. I stayed at home for a week, doing not very much except fretting.

I watched the TV news on tenterhooks. There were grainy satellite pictures of Chernobyl every night. The stomach-turning footage of the fire still glowing in the reactor's heart. Pictures of tiny helicopters tipping Lilliputian buckets of sand over the flames of Hell in an attempt to extinguish them. News of how the news was being fed to the Russian people was being fed to us. The Russian government had belatedly admitted the occurrence of an accident at Chernobyl, Pripyat, in which two people had lost their lives. We in the west knew better than that. We patted ourselves on the back. But what did we really know? We knew what our government and our media chose to tell us. That put us in the same boat as the Russians. How much of the truth about the disaster was being withheld from *us?* After all, even I was being economical with the truth – or with what I thought might be the truth – about it.

I asked my parents if anyone had tried to contact me. Doctor Cotton had phoned twice, they told me. The first time to explain what had happened to me, the second to ask if my parents had any further news. Unavailingly. The Foreign and Commonwealth Office in London had been the first to announce the news of my extended stay in the USSR... But anybody else? I queried hopefully. Any of my friends? The answer was no.

Dickon had said he'd try and get my phone number from either David Cotton or from Jenny. Perhaps he'd meant after the start of the university term. But then I'd be back at university too, and my parents' home number would be no use to him at all. As for me trying to phone Dickon – I hadn't got his phone number either. That chaotic morning at the Leningrad station in distant Moscow.

I spent my week of convalescence in a sort of half-life. Still weak from my illness but recovering a little day by day. I returned to the village doctor and he pronounced me well enough to tackle the long train journey to Durham the next day. I reminded him I'd made a much longer journey by plane a week ago. He said, in a very fatherly way, 'Just being careful with you. As they were in Moscow.'

I caught the train to London and went from Charing Cross to Kings Cross by tube. There was time to kill before my train. I wandered into the station bar. Across the not very crowded room a dark-haired young man sat all alone, perched on a high stool with a lonely glass of beer. He was wearing his black winter coat, pulled up around his ears, although the late April day was mild. Deep in my chest my heart did something I'd never felt it do before. I walked quickly, almost ran, towards the young man. Almost unable to believe I was doing it I shouted out his name.

SEVENTEEN

Dickon looked at me blankly for a micro-second, then his smile broke out of him like the sun blazing out from behind a cloud.

His face had changed. He'd lost weight. In just a fortnight. He slid gracefully off his stool and we met standing. We embraced for a second, chest to chest, but the place was a bit too public for a man-to-man kiss. He said, 'Oli, you've lost weight.'

I said, 'So have you.' Then I realised that I'd changed in another way in the last brief fortnight. I'd grown up. But I couldn't say this. I couldn't say anything. Everything wanted to come out at once: my love for Dickon; the complication of Dmitri and the things we'd done and said; the Chernobyl dimension. The thoughts bottlenecked in my mind, the words jammed in my throat. I started to cry instead.

'Don't cry,' Dickon said, trying to smile as he said it.

'You're crying too,' I said.

He said, 'I got the measles. I guess that's what you had. That's why I couldn't get in touch.'

'You're going up to Edinburgh? Are you strong enough? I'm terribly sorry… You caught it from me, of course…'

'You're going up to Durham…?'

'On the Edinburgh train in twenty minutes…'

'We don't have to go today. We could stay in London overnight…'

'Don't know where… Who with…'

'We could…'

'I've a better idea,' I said. 'Break your journey in Durham. Stay with me overnight.' I knew that I wouldn't want to let him continue on to Edinburgh tomorrow if he did that, but we would cross that bridge when we came to it.

I saw Dickon think very quickly for half a second, then he said, 'OK. We'll do that.'

'I'll get myself a beer,' I said.

He said, 'No. I'll get it.' Then he rumpled the top of my head.

We talked all the way up. All the four hours it took to hurtle north, past Doncaster, York and Darlington, to the small city in which I had a room and a small bed in which we would spend the night.

187

Dickon wanted to know what I knew about Chernobyl. I told him some of it. For reasons of my own I was a bit sparing with the truth. I told him about Dmitri. Again I was niggardly with the facts. I told him how our brief friendship had kept me from going stark raving mad with loneliness. I didn't tell him that Dmitri was distraught at the disappearance of his parents after the Chernobyl accident. I didn't tell him that the two of us had had sex. I told Dickon about the inspiring example of stoical determination that had been set me by Bruce, the spider in the bath.

Dickon told me how he'd begun to feel ill on the plane from Moscow to London. How, after a night in his own bed at home he had not felt better but much worse. How he'd gone to the doctor, been given the same diagnosis that I'd been given in Moscow and been sent home to bed for a few days. This was only his third day up.

I repeated my apology for passing the virus on to him. He brushed it aside. 'That happens when you get close to people. It's part of life. It was only measles; not the AIDS virus.'

'Actually,' I said, 'I'd had measles when I was a kid. I didn't think you could get it again. My doctor said he thought it must have been a different strain.'

'Same here,' said Dickon. 'And that's exactly what my own doctor said.'

There was something wonderful about this discovery

that we'd shared an almost identical experience. I did hope, though, that nobody had had sex with Dickon while he was confined to his sick bed. The illogical jealousy of the cheating partner.

The train ran through a long cutting just south of Durham. Its emergence from it onto a long high viaduct made the first sight of the city all the more dramatic. The cathedral and castle perch next to each other on the crown of a hill and, from the curve of the viaduct, appear to revolve gradually as the train slows for the station stop.

'It's nearly as good as Edinburgh,' Dickon admitted reluctantly, still peering at the view as he hauled his case down from the rack. 'I admire it every time I come past. But first time I'm stopping off here.'

We shared a taxi. The road from the station to the castle was not long, but it dropped very steeply to the river, then wound even more steeply up to the hilltop. Both still convalescing, we didn't feel like walking it.

I signed Dickon in as a dinner guest in the castle's great hall, then took him up the eighty-nine steps to my small bedroom. We laid our suitcases on the floor (together they almost filled the space) then, without taking our coats off, we started to kiss. It was like being back in Russia. A re-run of that first time in Suzdal. The first time in Leningrad. Now, the first time in Durham. And, like those two other first times, after the first overflow of pent-up kisses had run its course, we got undressed together.

I had never fucked Dickon, though back in Leningrad he had done me once. Now I wanted to, but somehow I couldn't do it yet. Perhaps I wasn't ready for it. Perhaps neither of us was up to it; we were still recovering from an illness we'd both had very recently. I told Dickon I wanted to fuck him, but that somehow this didn't seem the right moment. He said he understood that. I had another worry too, of course, that was connected with Dmitri, but I wasn't going to go into that. At least, not yet.

And Dickon said he wasn't up for fucking me either. I said I understood that. We lay together naked on top of my bed. We enjoyed the reunion of our tough young arms and legs, and necks, and cocks, and chests. And heads. And hands. And feet. Lying on our sides, tummies intermittently pressed together, we used our hands to bring each other off. Dick came explosively. First for once. His spunk came out of him so energetically and so copiously that it coated my neck and chest. I'd never seen him go quite like that. I couldn't help remembering Dmitri's fountain spurt that day – ten days ago – back in the hospital, and as far removed from this time and place as Shangri-La or Planet Zog. I tried to banish thoughts of Dmitri. In fairness to Dickon. In fairness to me. In fairness to us. But it was monumentally difficult to do that.

I came a moment later. Much more modestly. Just a tiny splash in fact. But Dickon seemed more than pleased with my effort, and wrapped me tightly in his arms in a warm and wet cuddle.

We snoozed for a bit, burrowing beneath the covers for warmth, then, when we awoke it was time for dinner. We dressed, walked down the eighty-nine steps, across the courtyard and into hall, up a few more, grander, steps.

'Brace yourself for sarky comments,' I told Dick.

'I'm braced,' he said.

But none came. At least not in our presence. Instead I was treated as a bit of a hero. A lot of people wanted to crowd around and hear of my adventures. If I'd brought back a souvenir of my far-flung travels in the pleasing shape of an Edinburgh undergrad called Dickon ... well, everyone seemed fine with that. Even Mo. Perhaps especially Mo, who made sure in the scramble for seats that he ended up sitting next to the two of us. Dinner was roast beef with Yorkshire pudding and horseradish sauce. It was like an official confirmation of the fact that I was back in Durham, England.

'We really ought to go and see Jenny,' I said as the meal ended and we all got up – all three hundred of us – to file out of the Great Hall.

'Yes,' said Dickon. He paused. 'Yes, we ought.' He paused again.

'I know exactly what you mean,' I said.

'We could do that in the morning,' he said, as though he'd come up with an idea that was extremely bright.

'Yes we could,' I said.

'Well, well, well,' called a nearby voice. Filing down the outside steps among us was David Cotton. We'd seen him in dinner, sitting far away from us on the dais at high table. Now he joined us. 'I saw you both in dinner,' he told us. 'The return of the Prodigal,' he said to me. Then to Dickon, 'Have you come back to the wrong university by mistake?'

'There was method in my madness,' Dickon said. David smiled at that.

'Come and have a nightcap with me later,' David said. 'I want to hear your adventures.' He took his gold fob watch from his breast pocket and looked at it. 'Only a small nightcap, mind. Say, nine o'clock. That'll give you a chance to go on afterwards and have a proper nightcap elsewhere.'

We thanked him and our routes diverged in the crowd as it dispersed in the courtyard; we joined the part of it that jostled out through the Norman gate.

There was time before nine o'clock for me to give Dick a short tour of the central core of the city. The Old and New Bailey, those cosily wriggly contiguous Georgian streets. The path that led down to Prebends' Bridge among the woods by the river. The old lamps were beginning to come on in the spring dusk as we made our way along the bank-side path and then zigzagged our way back up beneath the cathedral's beetling battlements, past the Music School and onto

Palace Green.

David's suite of rooms were conveniently placed, halfway between ground level and my eyrie in the lofty keep. There were forty-two steps up to it – and of course forty-seven above. His study cum living room was comfortably furnished. A glowing Persian rug brightened the floor and a clavichord stood beneath the window. I knew of no student who had dared to ask him to entertain them on it.

David was still in bow tie and sports jacket. He poured us all a small glass of dry Madeira and we sat around in armchairs politely sipping it. One of the first things David asked Dickon was, 'Have you seen Jenny yet?' When we told him that that particular reunion was scheduled for the following morning I could almost see the cogs of speculation and deduction whirling in David's academic head. Then we went through the inevitable agenda. My escapade in Moscow. Dickon's brush with the measles virus. (Had any of the rest of our party gone down with it? we asked David. Not that he knew of, he said. All the Durham crowd were accounted for, and had made it to Durham for the start of term.) And we talked about Chernobyl, of course. As we went through that item (for the umpteenth time in my case) clouds of unease mushroomed into my mind. And an idea came to me in the fallout. Though it wasn't one I was going to go public with tonight.

When the tiny glasses of Madeira were empty they stayed that way. After a couple of minutes it was very evident that they would not be replenished tonight.

Dickon and I looked at each other, nodded, rose from our comfortable seats and said goodnight.

'Well, have a safe journey to Edinburgh tomorrow,' David said to Dickon as he gave his hand a farewell shake. 'Though I can't help feeling it's au revoir only. I'm guessing that you'll soon be back.' He didn't say why he guessed that, or who he supposed would be the reason for any future visits, and we didn't help him out.

'Do you want to go out for one?' I asked Dickon when we again stood alone together on the stone steps – forty-two descending and forty-seven going up.

'Do you?' Dick queried, peering searchingly into my eyes.

'Not especially,' I said.

'I wouldn't mind…' Dickon felt his way through the sentence diffidently '… I wouldn't mind … just going back to bed.' And that, despite the fact that it wasn't much past nine-thirty, was what we did.

In the morning we didn't want to get up. Didn't want to leave each other's familiar naked body. Didn't want to leave that familiar warmth, that familiar hardness and softness, that familiar scent. But in the end we did.

It was permitted, and very usual, to sign in guests for dinner; but not for breakfast. Dickon and I joined a small throng of people heading into the Great Hall, and parked ourselves among a chattering breakfast group. 'Just talk to him as though he's always here,' I said to the others and they obliged wonderfully, and somehow none of the waitresses noticed the unknown extra face amongst us.

Jenny saved us the trouble of walking all the way out of town to her distant college by appearing on Palace Green, between the castle and the cathedral, just as we were setting out. 'I heard you were both here,' she said, and we all kissed. We went to a coffee shop to talk and catch up, then Jenny went off to a lecture which – as luck would have it – I didn't have to attend myself.

Then I walked with Dickon to the station. We took it in turns to carry his case. Remembering another walk with a suitcase, along a station platform that seemed would never end … on Moscow's Leningrad station. Our parting grew nearer, along with Durham's station and the looming high viaduct that led into it. We had almost reached the station entrance…

'I'm going to come back down at the weekend,' Dickon said. He rattled the words out quickly, as though he feared he'd lose confidence if he took his time about it. 'That is, if…'

'There's no if,' I said, cutting him off before his nerve had time to fail him. Then I heard a new grown-up strength and certainty in my own voice as I said, 'It's what I want.'

'Good,' said Dickon. It came out as a sigh of relief.

Dickon's ticket would have allowed him to break his

journey overnight in London but not in Durham. We'd got off the train yesterday easily enough; there had been nobody on the gate. Now we had to choose our moment. We waited till a small knot of people was about to go through, brandishing tickets at the man who guarded the platform entrance. 'Go now,' I said. 'Join that lot.'

'Yep. I'll be back Saturday midday. Where will you...?'

'Meet in the Shakespeare pub,' I said. 'We just passed it. I'll be there from when it opens. Twelve o'clock....'

'Will do. Better get myself into the middle of that little lot...'

Childish panic overcame me. 'We still haven't said...'

'I know,' he said, now walking rapidly towards the group of travellers, hauling his suitcase. 'We will...' He had to leave me then, if he wasn't going to have to buy a second ticket. There wasn't time for a farewell hug or kiss.

We hadn't said what, though? We would... would what? I watched Dickon make it safely through the gate, protected by that little knot of strangers, waving his ticket just too far away from the inspector's eyes for him to read the details on it. I saw him lug his suitcase up and over the footbridge. I watched him standing alone on the opposite platform. From time to time he waved to me. He smiled too, a bit forlornly, every time he looked at me. I waved to him and smiled at him, as often as seemed reasonable. Then his train pulled in and he

196

disappeared behind it. The train pulled out again a minute later, leaving an empty platform behind it like a piece of magic.

I turned and began to walk down the hill. I didn't know what the fuck I was going to do between now and Saturday. I felt as though my heart was going to burst.

EIGHTEEN

It was true that I had no lectures that morning. But I had one in the afternoon. It was given, as it happened, by David Cotton. It was one of his series of lectures on medieval England. This one dealt with the importance of the Cistercian order of Benedictine monks in the national economy of the period; in particular the rearing of sheep and the trade in wool with the Continent.

At the podium, vested in his academic gown, with bow tie and watch-chain shining out beneath, he was very much Doctor Cotton rather than my fellow traveller and hotel roommate Michael, with whom Dickon and I had sipped Madeira the previous night. He lectured quietly, without big gestures or hyperbolic rhetoric, yet you could have heard a pin drop in the lecture room as he brought the period to life in front of us using nothing but words to paint his pictures with.

He described the white stone skeletons of the big abbeys down in Yorkshire – Rievaulx, Fountains, Jervaulx – gaunt and hollow as today they stood. Then he clothed them with the flesh of the life that was lived there in the past. He talked of the huge abbey churches that hummed like beehives on great feast days; of the bare and spartan dormitories with their communal washrooms; of the refectories where meals were taken in silence, and of the parlours, where – as the name might indicate – the sheep-rearing inmates could talk. He went on to describe their farming methods, and their huge success – and the awkward embarrassment of their growing wealth. We all knew, of course, how the story ended – with Henry VIII closing down the industry, dispossessing its monastic labour force and pocketing the accumulated capital... David rounded off his lecture ... he had held us spellbound for an hour without the use of notes ... with a quote from Shakespeare. *'Bare ruin'd choirs, where late the sweet birds sang.'* Then he nodded his head minimally and neatly left the podium.

I caught him up outside. 'David... Can I talk to you about something?'

He stopped and turned to me. 'Of course, Oliver. What can I help you with?'

'It's a bit private actually,' I said, looking round at the two or three dozen students who we were walking out of the lecture halls with.

He said, 'I still have a little Sercial left. If you'd like to look in at nine o'clock...?'

I said I would and dismissed myself with a little hop and jump. Then I remembered something and turned back towards him. 'That was a very interesting lecture, by the way. We learned a lot.'

'Nine o'clock,' he said.

Sercial is the name of the driest kind of Madeira wine. The sweetest is the famous Malmesy. But there was something about the bright gold acerbic Sercial that seemed very right. I mean it seemed the right kind of liquor to be found in David's drinks cabinet.

I sat in the same chair as I'd done the previous night. 'Thank you,' I said as I took the proffered small glass.

'Now what is it you'd like to talk about?' David asked as soon as he'd taken his own chair.

I said, 'It's about radiation sickness.'

'Good heavens,' said David. 'I know I hold the title of Doctor, but I'm not the sort of doctor who's qualified to deal with that. Are you sure you've not mistaken me for someone else?'

I grinned at him as he had meant me to. 'I know,' I said. 'But there's really no-one else I can ask. It's sort of … intimate.'

'I see,' he said. Then he became serious and businesslike. 'You're thinking about Chernobyl, of course.'

'Yes,' I said. 'I know it was a long way from Moscow that it all happened, but… Well, the thing is, I think they may have brought some of the victims into the hospital I was in. Just temporarily. Just in the course of one night.'

'But you were in an isolation room,' David said carefully. 'I'm sure you were perfectly safe.'

I said, 'I did come into close contact with a doctor – the one who befriended me – I mentioned him last night

– and I worry that he might have had contact with those people … even though he said he didn't. I didn't want to worry Dick by mentioning this last night.'

'How close was this … er … conta…' He cut himself off. 'I'm sorry. I need to be more careful. I don't want to find myself asking questions I have no business to ask.'

'It's quite all right, David,' I said. 'I did bring the subject up. What I want to know – I'll try not to beat about the bush – is whether radioactivity is contagious in … er … intimate circumstances.'

David took a sip of his Sercial, then smiled at me. 'I'm no scientist, as you well know, but I'm as certain as any non-scientist can be that radiation is not a contagion. I imagine that you could become radioactive if you touched someone who was covered in radioactive fallout dust and then accidentally licked your fingers before washing them or something like that…' He smiled again. 'I'm quite certain that it's not something that can be passed on in the course of normal sexual contact. So I think you can relax about that.'

David looked at me very interrogatively. I stayed silent. David said, 'I will speak to Doctor Chessingham at breakfast. To make assurance double sure, as Shakespeare says. I'm quite sure, though, that his answer will be the same as mine is. I'll ask him. It'll be one of those *it happened to a friend* questions that we all put to expert professionals. Although, in the light of recent events he might be able to make a shrewd guess who I'm talking about.'

'I won't be too worried if he does,' I said. 'You've already reassured me more than you can imagine. Thank you so much...' I emptied my eyebath-sized glass and made a move to get up from my chair.

'Before you go,' David said. 'Dickon's coming back down from Edinburgh at the weekend. Did I understand that right?'

I said, 'You did.'

'To see the friends he made in Russia,' said David nodding. 'That's very nice. Though it'll hit his pocket hard if he makes a habit of it.'

'Well, he won't be coming every weekend,' I said. 'Some weekends I'll be going up to Edinburgh...' I stopped. I realised that I'd just put an end to any remaining uncertainty on David's part as to which of his tour group Dickon had got involved with. In a rather brazen tone I said, 'Well, that's how it is.' And shrugged.

'Well, good luck to you both,' he said. 'But a word of caution. Long-distance relationships are difficult to sustain for the long term. Especially when one is as young as you both are. I mustn't lecture you on the subject ... I've no business doing that ... but I think I should warn you to be prepared for all eventualities – even the bad ones.' He paused for a second. 'I wouldn't want you to... I wouldn't want you to break your heart.'

Then he got up from his chair and walked to the door with me. He gave me a brief handshake as we said goodnight.

The next morning brought something unprecedented. A note from David Cotton, in his unmistakeable neat, small fountain-pen handwriting, which I found in my pigeon hole when I went to check my post. It read:

Dear Oliver

Doctor Chessingham has added the weight of his informed opinion to my not unreasonable guess. There is next to no chance that you have anything to worry about. However, he has kindly invited you to present yourself at the Clarendon Room in the Physics department, out on the Science Site, at two o'clock this afternoon, where a group of his students can run a conclusive test. While I am as sure as Doctor Ch is that this will be quite unnecessary I feel sure you will be obliging enough to turn up at the appointed time and place and entertain his students.

Kind regards

David

I had never walked out to the Science Site. It was a little way from the town centre, in sight of fields and hedgerows and this sunny afternoon it made a pleasant trip.

I found the Clarendon Room quite easily. Its door stood open. Doctor Chessingham, whom I already knew well by sight, though we'd never spoken, was inside, talking informally to a group of students. I recognised some of them too. A couple were also in my college. I was slightly taken aback to see that everybody, including Doctor Ch, was wearing a white coat.

Doctor Chessingham turned at the sound of my entrance. 'Ah, there you are. Mister Patten, I presume?'

I said, 'Yes, Doctor Chessingham.'

He jerked his head towards the lecturer's imposing workbench. On top of it was a piece of equipment that was roughly the same size and shape as a car battery, wired up to the electricity main and with something resembling a telephone receiver attached by another wire to it. 'We are the proud possessors of a Geiger counter,' he told me. 'We don't often get a chance to use it. Would you like to stand just here so that everyone can see you?'

I stood where I was told to, next to the car battery thing on the desk. Actually, in fairness to the machine it looked less like a car battery than a battery charger. It had dials and controls on it. It was a notch more sophisticated.

'OK,' said Doctor Chessingham. 'Mr Strickland. Would you like to come up first?'

I didn't know Mr Strickland. He wasn't from my college. But he looked the same age as I was and seemed friendly enough. He smiled at me a bit nervously as he picked the telephone receiver thing up. I smiled much more nervously back. I heard Doctor Ch's voice beside me, addressing Mr Strickland. 'Start at the top. Work your way down and continue till you finish.'

And Mr Strickland, my fellow student with the unknown first name, did.

He ran the thing over the top of my head with trembling hands, then started on down my neck. I strained my ears to hear the clicking sound I'd heard in sci-fi films. There came not a peep. Strickland was running the thing up and down my chest. My back. It felt extraordinarily intimate. The more so because Mr Strickland was an absolute dish. With blond hair, blue eyes, and Rugby-player's legs.

Legs. Strickland crouched down and ran the thing down my legs. His hands, which had stopped shaking with the realisation that by now there weren't likely to be any clicks, had started again as he slid his apparatus over my bum and crotch. But when he reached the relative safety of my knees and calves the shaking stopped. He finished up, on his knees, paying attention to my feet. 'Thank you Mr Strickland,' said Doctor Chessingham. Very well done. Next…'

One by one the students came up and ran the telephone-receiver thing over me. Not a sound came out of the machine. Not a pointer on any dial so much as trembled. The experience was very much like being frisked repeatedly by security at an airport. As physics student succeeded physics student in carrying out the test their friendly smiles turned into grins which then grew broader. Each new student frisker now wore a grin that was broader than the last. I started to giggle and so did they. By the end of the experiment we were all laughing, including the great Doctor Ch himself.

'Well, I think we've proved conclusively that you've nothing to worry about,' he told me, summing the thing up. 'Whatever it was you were worried about. Anyway, thanks for coming along. You can run off now and get back to learning about Erasmus or Rasputin while we get back to more serious stuff.' He gave me a smile that made his eyes twinkle. 'Not that Erasmus and Rasputin aren't serious. I wouldn't want dear Doctor Cotton to think I'd said that.'

I walked out of the Clarendon Room and off the Science Site as if on buoyant air. I felt as relieved as if I'd just been found negative in an AIDS test.

I had a drink with Jenny that night. Bizarrely Mo joined us. But that was the nature of a small university like Durham. You chanced on a friend in the street while you were on your way to meet someone else and – provided the other party wasn't your girlfriend or boyfriend – they'd tag along and join you in the pub.

'You seem very bouncy tonight,' observed Jenny when we'd installed ourselves at a table in the lounge bar of the Three Tuns.

'Yes,' echoed Mo. 'Very Tiggerish.'

'It's because I've had a test done on me,' I said. 'I'm radiation-negative.' I told them the story of my afternoon's adventure on the Science Site.

'But you can't have been really worried,' Jenny said. 'When Chernobyl went up you were four hundred miles from the blast. The wind wasn't even going that way. The first we knew of it in the west was when radioactive stuff fell out of a cloud in Sweden.'

'The reindeer are positively glowing,' Mo said.

'I know,' I said. 'I wasn't worried really. It's just that … you know … you can't be too careful…'

'…When other people are involved.' Mo had finished my sentence in a way that I hadn't planned to.

'What do you mean by that?' I asked.

'Only joking,' he said. 'By the way, your friend's nice. The one you brought to dinner and then to breakfast. Dickon, have I remembered right?'

'Dinner and also breakfast?' Jenny echoed with an emphasis that was rather arch. I saw her beautiful eyebrows go eloquently up.

'Yes,' I said. 'Dickon's the name.'

'Frances Hodgson Burnett, The Secret Garden,' said Mo, and Jenny and he exchanged a complicit look.

'Nice name, Dickon,' volunteered Jenny. 'And a lovely children's book. We all got to know each other very well in Russia. Oli used to shorten his name to Dick.'

'I'm saying nothing,' I said.

NINETEEN

I didn't wait till the Shakespeare opened at midday that Saturday. I walked to the station soon after eleven and waited for the next train from Edinburgh to come in. I scanned the arriving passengers anxiously, excitedly... Then there he was.

'I couldn't wait till twelve o'clock,' I said. We hugged.

'I'm glad you couldn't.' he said. 'I didn't know how I was going to survive, myself.'

He just had a weekend backpack this time, not a big start of term suitcase. We walked back. We walked past the Shakespeare without giving it a glance; we didn't need a drink.

Arrived at the top of the eighty-nine steps, safely inside my little room and with the door shut, 'Can I fuck you?' I asked.

Dickon chuckled as we held each other tight. 'I was going to ask you the same thing but you got it in first. The question, I mean. You got the question in first.'

I laughed. We got undressed. I lay on top of Dickon. 'You're trembling,' I said.

'I've never been fucked before. You know that.'

'And neither had I before Leningrad,' I said. 'You

know that. But I'll be gentle, like you were with me. And if you want to stop at any time…'

'Just go for it,' Dickon said. He raised his knees and spread his legs.

I found his sphincter with a finger, then moistened it with a copious dispensation of pre-come that had just then spooled from the tip of my cock. (The timing of that had been perfect.) I felt Dick's muscles relax after a moment of my attentions and then, acutely conscious that I was crossing one of life's big thresholds, I tried to enter him with my prick.

It wasn't as easy as it had been with a finger. My cock, like Dickon's had (has) a broad head on it. But he had managed to get his into me without too much trouble and without hurting me much…

Suddenly I'd made it. To my astonishment my dick slipped straight inside him, disappearing up to the hilt. Dick grimaced his surprise for a second, then his face relaxed. And then … well, I was young, it was my first time … 'I'm going to come,' I said. My hips bucked and pounced upon him, seemingly of their own volition, and I felt myself empty out into Dickon's innermost physical space. I imagined I was making contact with his heart. The extraordinary, wonderful smile he gave me, looking up as he felt me burst inside him told me that I was.

'Now let me…' I said. I turned my attention, and my fingers to Dickon's straining erection and, without removing my own cock from his anus, brought him swiftly off. He came with great energy and abundance, covering his belly and chest with thick cords of white. We lay together for a minute, awed and silenced.

Then, 'That was special,' Dickon said.

'It certainly was.' I lay flat on his chest, bathing my own chest in his warm spunk.

'It wasn't just sex,' said Dickon.

'No,' I agreed. 'It was better than that.'

'More than that,' said Dickon.

'Yes, it was,' I said. 'Much more than that.' I withdrew my long penis from Dick's bottom and cleaned us both up.

Half an hour later we were dressed and on our way down the stone steps, then across the courtyard to the Great Hall for college lunch. I'd had the forethought to sign Dickon in as my guest in advance.

'We've been invited for dinner tonight by Jenny,' I told Dickon as we spooned our lunchtime soup beneath the portraits of Bishop Van Mildert and sundry others under the echoing hammer-beam roof. 'You, me and David and Michael and a couple of the other Moscow people.'

'In her college?' Dickon asked.

'She's just moved out of college,' I said. 'She's in a flat-share in South Street. Which you won't know, but it's high up on the riverbank opposite, with brilliant views of the cathedral and this place. Tonight's a sort of house-warming.'

'Well, that's the evening sorted,' Dickon said.

'So what are you guys doing this afternoon?' Mo interjected naughtily from across the table.

'Never you mind,' I told him.

Dickon said, 'We'll think of something, I expect.'

We did. We went for a walk. We walked out of the city along Crossgate Peth to Nevilles Cross. Then up to Crossgate Moor and out into the deep country towards Bearpark. I chose this lengthy route deliberately. I had much to say to Dickon and we would have a lot to deal with en route.

'I've had a test done,' I said suddenly. Wrenching the conversation away from whatever safe, ordinary subject we'd been talking about as our way took us up out of Durham's streets and into the rolling green countryside beyond them.

'What sort of test?' I heard Dickon's voice darken as he asked.

'A radioactivity test,' I said. 'I had myself checked out with a Geiger counter by the physics department.' I heard the words sounding absurd as I dropped them, as it were, at Dickon's feet.

'Why?' he asked unsurprisingly. 'You were nowhere near the accident.'

'I had reasons for being concerned,' I said. 'But it's OK. I'm not radioactive. Not remotely. Totally clear of any fallout.'

All over the western world these days gay men were having to tell their partners that they'd taken an AIDS test – many of them delighted to be able to say that they'd tested negative, but still having to go on and explain why they'd felt it necessary to take the test in the first place.

'So, your reason for being concerned?' Dick asked.

I told him about the nightmarish night in which the corridor outside my isolation room had seemed to fill with the maimed and sick survivors of the Chernobyl blast. I told him that I suspected Dmitri had been in contact with those people. Dick already knew that Dmitri and I had been close. That Dmitri had used to sit on the side of my bed... I told Dickon how I'd expressed my fears to David Cotton and how David had kindly arranged for me to have the unofficial yet conclusive test.

'Well that's all right then,' Dickon said.

'It is,' I said. 'And yet it isn't.'

'Mmm?' enquired Dick.

'There's something I have to come clean about.' I paused. Dickon didn't speak. The pause grew longer.

'I'm waiting,' Dickon said in a voice that tried to be neutral, but I could hear the fear in it.

I said, 'When we parted that morning in Moscow three weeks ago we'd only really just met. We'd had sex, I know. And something had happened between us…'

'Yep.'

'Something big. Yes. I know that. I knew it then. But…'

'But what?' Dickon asked. His voice was tight with a sort of dread.

'We hadn't made any promises to each other. Actually we still haven't. We hadn't made any claims on each other. Like being faithful … exclusive … anything like that.'

'No,' Dickon said. His voice was clenched.

'Something happened,' I said. 'Something between me and Dmitri.' I ran on quickly, before Dickon could interrupt. 'It was before things between you and me were as they are now. I didn't see myself as … belonging to anyone. I didn't see you as … belonging to me…'

'You had sex with Dmitri?' Dickon didn't sound angry. Just astonished. 'In a hospital bed?'

'That's about the size of it,' I said miserably. 'We didn't do what we've done today,' I went on, desperate to clutch at extenuating straws of circumstance. 'We didn't put our cocks in each other's mouth. We just...'

'Just what?' Dick's voice was cold and dead.

I took a big breath in an attempt to steady myself. 'He lay on top of me as I lay in bed. We put our cocks together...'

'Skin to skin or through your clothes?' Dickon wanted to know. With a fierce urgency. I hadn't known before today just how much detail the other person would want to know in the course of a conversation like this.

'Skin to skin,' I said abjectly. 'We both came rather spontaneously...'

'Over your bellies? Like us?'

I could only nod.

'I see,' said Dickon.

'Like I said,' I said, and my voice came out all primly, 'it was just a one-off.'

'But it happened,' said Dickon in a cool hard voice.

'Of course it fucking happened,' I said, angry suddenly. 'I wouldn't be telling you something I'd made up.'

We walked on in silence for what seemed like ages.

Inside I felt I was dying. All I could seize on was the thought that we were still walking along, side by side, in the spring sunshine, in the rolling Durham landscape. Larks were singing their scratchy songs above our heads. Neither of us had turned back towards the city. It was a small mercy. I was grateful for that.

Minutes passed. Then Dickon said, 'This Dmitri... What was he like?'

'Older than us,' I said. 'About ten years older. Good looking, actually. Not like you, of course...'

'Of course,' said Dickon. I thought I saw the ghost of a smile flit across his face. Though perhaps I only wishfully imagined it.

We walked on a bit more in silence. 'When I last saw Dmitri...' I was very unsure of myself as I began to say this, yet somehow I knew I had to say it. 'He wasn't happy...'

'Because he was saying goodbye to you...'

'That's another ... fuck it ... maybe ... but I was saying something else. His parents lived in Pripyat, the town that was built to house the workers of the Chernobyl plant. His father worked there. At the plant. He didn't know what had happened to them. Doesn't know if they're alive or dead. Couldn't get news of them. Then all those poor people at the hospital with radiation burns or whatever they had...'

Dickon spun towards me and buried me in his big

embrace. A word came from him quietly that nevertheless hit me like a bomb blast because it was the last thing I'd expected. 'Darling,' he said.

Nobody except my mother had ever called me that.

'I'm so, so sorry,' I said, and my voice broke.

Dickon just said, 'Don't…'

We clasped hands as we continued our walk. The way we'd done in Suzdal, out on the snowy ramparts, and in Leningrad as we found our way home in the small hours of Easter Day along Nevsky Prospekt.

'You haven't written to him yet?' Dickon checked when we were back in my room in the keep, glowing and tingling after our long country walk. 'You must.'

'I can't remember his surname,' I said.

'We can work on that.'

'He probably won't be able to write back,' I argued reasonably.

'Does it matter if he doesn't?' Dickon said. 'He may not even get your letter for that matter. But that doesn't mean you don't have to write it. It'll be like a message in a bottle. The chances of it coming ashore and being read by someone who'll understand it are remote. But even so…'

'I know what you mean,' I said.

We stood together at my small window and looked out. The keep rose a hundred feet above the city's rooftops. My view from it showed the wide countryside to the north-east: the notch in the hills ten miles away where the road cut through towards Sunderland, the gaunt pillars and pediment of the Penshaw Monument and the distant crags beyond it…

'I'll write something,' I said. 'I promise. It'll take me a while to put my thoughts in order. To find out what I want to write.'

'You might also think about what *he* might want you to write,' Dickon said.

'I see,' I said. We went on looking at the panorama spread beneath us in silence. The days were lengthening at a gallop. The early evening sun still made the sky sparkle and the green grass pulsate with life. After my internment in the Botkin I would never again take for granted the wonder of the world that was green grass. Not for as long as I had life.

'There's something else I ought to tell you,' I said.

Dickon laid his hand lightly around my shoulder. 'Go on,' he said. 'I'll brace myself.'

'When Dmitri told me about his parents … and we knew we were saying goodbye and would probably never meet again … it got a bit emotional… I mean, we both did.'

'Yep,' said Dickon. I could feel him bracing himself.

'I told him … a bit extravagantly … I mean, I didn't know what was going to happen. I didn't know we'd be here now…'

'Go on,' Dick said.

'I incautiously told him I'd like to live with him. He told me he'd like to live with me…'

'Of course,' said Dickon. 'Of course he did. Anyone would. Anyone who had any sense.' I felt his arm squeeze me tight.

'He told me he loved me. I told him the same thing…' I couldn't remember at this precise moment which of us had said it first. I decided not to raise the issue.

'I see,' said Dickon. His voice, which had been full of bounce and sparkle in the last few minutes now sounded punctured and flat.

'It wasn't that I didn't mean it…' I said. For the second time this afternoon I felt my voice break.

'No, of course,' said Dickon, striving to be reasonable about it.

'When I say a thing like that … I mean, I mean it. If I ever say it again to anyone… I'll mean it…'

Dickon turned me slowly towards him and kissed me on the lips. 'It's OK,' he said. Very softly he repeated it. 'It's OK, Oli.'

'Dickon, I love you,' I said.

There was a second's silence during which Dick and I just gripped each other tightly.

'I love you, Oli,' Dickon said.

'I'd like to live with you, Dickon,' I said.

'I want to live with you, Oliver,' Dickon said.

We stayed at the window, standing, rocking slightly in our embrace. Beyond the window pane the landscape vanished into a great, great distance where lay the North Sea and Denmark and the Baltic states, and the hundreds of miles of forest that lay beyond them and ran to Suzdal, Moscow and the magical city of Leningrad that had once been called St Petersburg.

TWENTY

I wrote my letter to Dmitri the following weekend, sitting in the train on the journey north to Edinburgh. It was a difficult letter to write anyway, even without the scenery beyond the train window that kept distracting me from the task.

I had never been to Edinburgh. I'd never the taken the train north from Durham any further than Newcastle. Once it left that sprawling city it headed, I discovered, across high wild moorland towards the sea, then followed the craggy coastline all the way up to the Scottish border.

Dear Dmitri

I don't know if this letter will ever find you, but I hope it does.

I want to thank you for...

I had to break off. The wonderful sight of Bamburgh Castle, perched on its crag at the edge of the sea had caught my attention and now held me in its thrall.

I told you I lived in a castle. Well, I'm writing this

letter on board a train that s just passing another castle, that sits beside the Northumbrian sea like a castle in a fairytale. It's like something from the Arthurian legend – extravagantly romantic and beautiful.

I'm on a train because I'm on my way to see Dickon in Edinburgh, where he studies, as I told you. It was you who told me to find Dickon again. Well, I have. And we…

Bamburgh Castle hadn't stayed framed in the window for all the time it took me to write that. I was looking across a wide bay at the equally magical island of Lindisfarne, with its tide-covered causeway, ruined abbey, and castle perched on a more than Disney-esque rock peak.

…we think we are somehow meant for each other. That is a cliché. But most of life is made up of clichés, it seems to me. That's why they become clichés. It's just that some clichés are sad ones and others are happy ones.

I have told Dickon all about you. And I mean all. He understands. He knows how important you are to me and that you always will be.

He was upset when I told him that you had lost contact with your parents and about the circumstances. I too remain unhappy about that. I do hope that by now you may have found them and they are OK.

You try not to write in clichés, but then...

We crossed the River Tweed on the Royal Border Bridge and peered down through the town and harbour of Berwick at the open sea.

I don't know if we shall ever meet again. I just want you to know I'll never forget you. I hope that, even in the difficult circumstances of Russian life, you will meet a man who you can find happiness with.

I love you always.

Your little Oliver

The letter was a bit of a muddle. I re-drafted it on a new sheet of paper, piecing together the ideas like the pieces of a jigsaw puzzle. Meanwhile we were nearly there. The train had stopped heading north, had followed the sharp turn of the coast at Dunbar and was heading west to Edinburgh. The final castle of the journey came into view (there had been Warkworth, Alnwick and Dunstanburgh even before Bamburgh) and we glided into Waverly station in its trench below the Royal Mile, midway between the Castle Rock and the Palace of Holyrood.

Dickon approved the letter. With my permission he wrote *Love from Dickon* at the end of it.

I had the address of the Botkin Hospital. It was on the discharge paper that I'd been issued with when I left. It was written in Cyrillic script, which we painstakingly copied onto the envelope. After all, the address would be read by Russian postal workers once it got there. The only bit we needed to write in western letters was Moscow USSR.

Well, there was another bit. Dmitri had shown me how to write his name in Cyrillic, and I wrote it now. But I still didn't remember his surname. Yet a funny thing happened at the moment I wrote Doctor Dmitri on the envelope. 'It's Stepanov,' I said. 'It's suddenly come to me. He's Doctor Dmitri Stepanov.'

'I'm impressed,' said Dickon. 'But memory does sometimes work like that.' I wrote Dmitri's surname on the envelope.

By the time I had to leave Edinburgh on Monday morning it wasn't just Dickon I didn't want to be parted from, it was the city he lived in too. I'd known in advance that Edinburgh was made for me to fall in love with, and that prediction had come true. I loved the cobbled streets of the old town, its crooked narrow ways and wynds. I loved the restrained Georgian grandeur of the New Town – where Dickon shared a high-ceilinged flat with a couple of fellow students. I loved the view up the Forth from the top of Arthur's Seat, with the two great bridges coming and going among the clouds. I loved the cakes, the haggis, the whisky, and the interior of Ryrie's Bar. I loved the pies.

I would be back in a fortnight, I told myself, as I sat on the train, doing the spectacular seaside journey in reverse. And I would see Dickon again in just five days, when it was his turn to come down to Durham for the weekend. But in the meantime my narrow single bed would feel vast and empty – occupied for five nights by only me.

And the cost of all this travelling to and fro… I was discovering one of life's great truths: falling in love is one of the quickest ways to dispose of your savings. And income too, presumably, if you had an income. But I was a student still. I didn't have one of those.

That summer term fell into a routine. Our weekends alternated between Durham and Edinburgh, a hundred and twenty miles apart, along the edge of the North Sea. Those expensive train journeys back and forth, castle following fairytale castle in sight of the sparkling blue. Get-togethers at Jenny's place in South Street on Dickon's weekends down with me. We'd walk up there with David – and Michael (Doctor Peters of the maths department) – and join the little group of ten Durhamites who'd been to Russia together and returned all slightly changed in our different ways.

In Edinburgh there'd be picnics in Holyrood Park... It wasn't your typical town park. More like the Lake District in miniature, or the Yorkshire Moors... Late night parties with Dickon's friends. The northern summer days were long, the nights – in Edinburgh especially – grew vanishingly small. Like the grasshopper in the fable we celebrated the long days. The grasshopper rubbed his legs together, and so did we. Our cocks too, and every other part of our physical and non-physical anatomies.

No happiness is perfect, though, and a distant cloud still shaded ours. No reply came to my letter to Dmitri. We didn't know what had happened to his parents – or to him. We heard news from Chernobyl – via our own TV and radio news. The still smouldering reactor was being encased in concrete. Entombed. Sarcophagus Chernobyl. The hopes that were pinned on the new broom in the Kremlin, Mikail Gorbachev, were dashed. The cost of Chernobyl emptied the Russian treasury as thoroughly as had done the First and Second World Wars.

As I write this, five years on, I know what I didn't then. That the economic cost of Chernobyl – forget for a moment the fathomless human cost – bankrupted the Soviet Union and caused it to implode. That the events of 1989 – including the rush to independence by the satellite states of Eastern Europe and the Baltics – were the direct results of the explosion of a nuclear power plant that happened on April 26th 1986 while I lay in a hospital just four hundred miles away, making love with

Dmitri.

David collared me one afternoon in June as I was walking across Palace Green towards the University Library. 'Would you like to call and see me this evening?' he asked in his quiet and scholarly way. 'It's about your work. Mainly. But I think I might be able to run to a glass of Madeira or two.'

I said yes, and thank you. I was particularly intrigued by the idea of a glass of Madeira or two. One glass was quite a usual thing these days, in David's sitting room in the castle, halfway up the monumental flight of stone stairs.. Sometimes with David and Dickon, sometimes just David and me. But it always was just the one glass. It had never been two.

I was taken aback, when I'd knocked at David's door and he'd said come in and I'd done that, to find him sitting in his armchair leafing through my latest essay. It was on the subject of the foreign policy of Edward IV. Edward IV, you will recall, spent his entire reign fighting England's internal War of the Roses, either from the throne when he was on it, or from a cell in the Tower of London when he wasn't and Henry VI was. I had never imagined him as having much time for foreign policy. It hadn't been easy for me, even with the resources of Palace Green library at my disposal, to get much of an idea of what it was.

'It's a bit thin,' David said without getting up from his

chair. 'Help yourself to Madeira.' He gestured vaguely. 'It's over there.'

'Thank you,' I said. I poured a glass for David and one for me.

'It's very woolly,' David said, continuing to peruse my pages with a frown.

'I don't see how a thing can be woolly if it's also thin,' I objected, handing my tutor his small glass of wine.

'Don't be pedantic, Oliver. Ah – thank you. You know exactly what I mean.'

I raised my own small glass to my lips and said cheers. David did likewise.

'You need to be more rigorous. More sedulous. More...'

'I get the point,' I said.

David dropped my essay onto the floor and turned to face me. He looked me quite sharply in the eye. 'How are things with Dickon and you?'

I said, 'They're fine.'

'Good,' he said. 'I'm glad. But ... dare I tell you? ... no I daren't, but I'm your tutor so it's part of my job... Here goes... It's always good at the beginning. Love. Falling in love. Being in love. But there comes a time ... well, you may know this already ... when the sexy gilt comes off the workaday gingerbread. It happens to every relationship…'

'It won't happen to ours…'

'As everyone in your position has always said and always will. But when it does…'

'It won't.'

'If it does…'

'It's only if.'

'Supposing, for the sake of argument…'

'OK. For the sake of argument,' I said tiredly. I knew by know that with David you could never win.

'Supposing, for the sake of argument,' said David, 'you found yourself one day with an older Dickon who was bald and not too steady on his pins – say in forty years' time. With someone who having sex with was no longer a delight but a routine – or maybe didn't happen at all, would you…?'

'I know what you mean,' I said slowly. I'd sort of gone through this in my mind sometimes, but very vaguely. I now felt challenged by hearing David spell it all out in this way. Yet somehow also honoured by his taking the trouble to do so. I didn't think I'd ever heard the word sex on his lips before.

'I'll try to answer you,' I said. I heard my voice tremble. Like a sand-reed under the onslaught of the wind that rushes up from the sea. 'I can't know. I can't know the future. No-one can. But as far as I can be sure – as far as anyone of my age can – I would still love Dickon, even then, and he'd love me.'

I saw something in David's face that I'd never seen there before. 'Well done,' he said slowly. 'Well spoken. And you're right. Of course no-one can know. But wanting it to be like that… That's the first footstep on the long road.'

I found I'd downed my Madeira rather quickly. 'Is it OK if I top myself up a bit?' I asked. I topped up both our glasses.

'Apologies for being a bit personal,' David said after a moment during which we digested what we'd both just said. 'But I needed to know. For a particular reason. Not just idle, prurient curiosity. The University of Newcastle is setting up a new course next year. It's in Russian language, history and literature. Two days a week. It's not full time because the idea is to recruit students who are already engaged in other studies at Newcastle … and elsewhere.' David stopped and looked at me very penetratingly. 'Interestingly, the history, languages and politics departments of various universities in northern England and in Scotland have been approached to see if any students of theirs… I naturally thought of Dickon and you.'

'Oh wow,' I said. 'Oh my God…'

'And there would be a travel allowance payable to

students from universities outside Newcastle. Though of course,' David went on smoothly, 'selection would rather depend on the recommendations of individual students' academic tutors...'

'Oh my God,' I said again. 'Do you think you would be prepared to recommend me?'

'Hmm,' said David. 'That might depend rather on how well you pulled your socks up in your next essay.' Then he smiled at me.

DASVIDANYA

So, five years on from that time, here we are. Dickon and I learned Russian at Newcastle. And the history of the great country of Russia too. What with time at Newcastle and weekends at Edinburgh and Durham we managed to be together for most of the rest of our university days. We took deep breaths and told our respective parents about ourselves. They were all fine about it once they'd had a little time to digest the inevitably rather difficult news. Then we were able to be together for much of the vacations too.

We'd caught the Russian bug big time. We applied – graduate entry – to the Foreign and Commonwealth Office and sat the exams. We made it clear where we wanted to work, and that we wanted to be posted together, not hundreds of miles apart. If they didn't like that idea they could lump it, we told them. In diplomatic terms.

I've written: here we are. Here is the elegant Black Sea port and tourist city of Odessa in Ukraine. Ukraine is a different place from Russia – at least for now. It was part of the Russian Empire, and part of the USSR, but is currently a separate country. Perhaps one could say it has had a similar relationship with Russia as Ireland has had with England – that is to say: complex in the extreme. But just as English is the principal language used in Ireland, so Russian is spoken in Ukraine.

We work in a British diplomatic outpost here. It's a bit of a juggling act. The Russian Bear breathes down our neck from just a few miles away: the breath sometimes hot, sometimes cold. But the climate here is seldom cold. Summers are hot and winters mainly mild. The city and the Black Sea coast are beautiful. And life was never meant to be simple anyway.

We have made several attempts to contact Dmitri over the years. To no avail. Although work has taken us to Moscow several times. The healing process and the grieving process that followed the Chernobyl catastrophe are still ongoing things, and involve both Russia and Ukraine. We tried to contact Natasha too, but with no better results than in the case of Dmitri. However – you never know what the future holds.

Dickon and I are happy together. Working together. Living together. That's the best ending to any story that I could possibly imagine. If we should meet our end together... Well, in a way that would be another good ending, since everything and everyone will meet their end one day. But – to be positive in the final sentence of this memoir – let that not be for a very, very long time yet. For we have much to do before we die, and far to go.

THE END

****

Other books by Adam Wye are **Love in Venice** and **Boy Next Door.**

About the Author

Adam Wye is a pen-name of the British author **Anthony McDonald**. (You can find Anthony McDonald's author page on Amazon, with information about the books he has written under his own name. Or click the link to his website below.) Under the name Adam Wye he is creating a new series of Gay Romance novels, light and sexy. **Gay Romance: Boy Next Door**, **Gay Romance: Love in Venice**, and **Gay Romance: Moscow '86** are the first three in the series. More to follow in the years ahead!

www.anthonymcdonald.co.uk

Made in the USA
Las Vegas, NV
19 April 2021